ASSIGNMENT PRAGUE

By

Helen Haught Fanick

For Vern and Margie

ACKNOWLEDGMENTS

My thanks to the family members and friends who have given me endless support, encouragement and love in my writing endeavors. Special gratitude is due the writers in my family, who also give me the benefit of their experience and wisdom. I appreciate those who have critiqued my work and offered suggestions and corrections—Ed Fanick, Ben Rehder, and Vernon and Marguerite Shettle. Thanks also to pixelstudio for the cover design. Historians may notice that I've taken a few liberties with the facts, but after all, this is fiction.

TABLE OF CONTENTS

CHAPTER ONE

The halfmoon wasn't providing much light, but Anton Janak could see by the light of the torches outlining the field that the parachute wasn't going to open. The woman didn't scream; the only sound was the fading drone of the unidentifiable plane as it headed back to England. She appeared to be working with the cords of the chute. His contact had told him she was cool under pressure, probably to silence his complaints about working with a woman, and he felt a twinge of embarrassment that his heart felt as if it were pounding a hole in his chest. There was nothing he and the others could do but stand and watch as she plummeted toward the ground.

He had warned his contact about the large oak in the middle of the field. Now it might be her salvation. She had the chute partially open and seemed to be maneuvering toward the tree.

"She's going to land in the tree," Erik murmured. "God help her." He crossed himself.

They ran toward the tree just as the woman crashed through the upper foliage and disappeared to the sound of splintering branches. Anton could see her slumped in a fork of the tree amid a tangle of cord and torn parachute.

"Get the blanket out of the back of the car. I'll get her down." Anton grabbed the lowest branch and pulled himself up so that his feet were on the limb and he was moving higher, beginning to climb. He reached the woman and felt for a pulse. "She's unconscious, but she's still alive."

He took a knife from his pocket and began cutting the harness and tangled cords. Her left leg dangled at a strange angle, and he was sure it was broken, but regardless, he had to get her out of the tree. He began lowering her as gently as possible, going down one limb at a time, until she was low enough for the others to reach her.

"I think her left leg's broken. Hold it steady and lay her on the blanket till I can get the chute out of the tree. We can't leave it here. Jakub, take your shirt off and try to stop the bleeding. I could feel blood seeping through the jump suit. You'll have to undo both the zippers to get her out of the suit. Take her helmet off, too. When you've stopped the bleeding, wrap the blanket around her. She's undoubtedly in shock."

Anton cut and ripped until he had freed the parachute from the grasping twigs. He dropped it to the ground, and then shined his flashlight around in the tree to see if he'd missed anything. He descended to the lowest limb and swung down. At that moment they heard a plane in the distance.

"The torches!" Jakub said, and they rushed to the car for the water in the trunk. They quickly doused the four blazes, threw the wet torches into the woods, and ran to hide under the tree till the plane was gone.

"I don't think they saw anything," Erik said. He was gathering up the shredded parachute, checking with his flashlight to make sure no trace was left on the ground. He shined the light up into the tree. "Do you suppose a pilot flying overhead in daylight could see that something fell into the tree and broke the branches?"

Anton was kneeling beside the woman. "I hope not. Maybe they'll think lightning hit it. We have to get her into the car. Let's lay her out on the backseat. The bleeding's under control for now, but it may start up again when we move her."

"I'll walk home from here," Erik said. "It's not that far."

"That's okay, you can ride. I'll have to get in the back with her to make sure she doesn't start bleeding again."

"Where are we going to take her?" Jakub asked. "We can't take her into town like this."

"We could say she was hit by a car when she was riding her bicycle," Erik said.

Anton shook his head. "I don't think that's going to work. She wouldn't be out riding her bike in the middle of the night. Then, too, these gashes don't look like they were made by being hit by a car, and if we're stopped, it could mean disaster." He looked at Erik. "I don't suppose we could—"

Erik looked at the ground. "No. My parents wouldn't agree to have her there. I'm sorry, but they're scared to death all the time."

Anton nodded. "I understand. Everybody's afraid. But we have to do something. I'm thinking that abandoned farm down near the highway is the only choice. The house is boarded up tight, and someone might notice if we broke in, but there's the barn. It's standing wide open. I checked it out the other day for possible use in emergencies. She'll only be there long enough for us to get her patched up. Then we'll move her into town."

"What if she wakes up in the barn? She won't know where she is. Who knows if she'll remember anything?"

"I'll have to stay with her," Anton said. "There's no other way."

Jakub smirked. "That's not going to make her highness happy."

Anton stood up, and Jakub backed away, holding out his hands up in a placating gesture. "I was just kidding. Take it easy."

"This is serious," Anton said. "The whole operation is in jeopardy because of a parachute failing to open, and you're making jokes."

Jakub didn't say anything for a minute, and then leaned over toward the woman. "What did you say her name is?"

"Tereza Valentova. Let's get her to the car."

The ancient Citroen Rosalie sedan was parked where the dirt road ended at the edge of the field. It had been yellow with black fenders, and had sat in his Teta Adelka's garage for years, taken out only for church on Sunday and an occasional shopping trip. She had protested, but not too strongly, when Anton took over the car, promising to show up on Sundays to take her to church and to be available when she needed to go shopping. He bought black paint and a brush and covered the yellow with black, also promising to return the car to its original yellow when the war was over.

Adelka Janakova was his father's older sister. Anton knew she never forgave the Germans for the death of her brother, his father, who died of a heart attack on the day the Nazis invaded Czechoslovakia. Anton didn't explain why he needed the car, but he was sure she had her suspicions and that part of her applauded. The other part undoubtedly worried about his safety.

She probably worried, too, that he was spending far less time at his law practice. Not that money was a problem—they both had trust funds from Anton's grandfather that covered necessities and more—but she believed he needed his work to make his life meaningful and often told him so.

Now his days were often spent away from his office, and there was no way he could explain what he was up to. The car was a necessity for him. He hoped, if she suspected he was part of the resistance, she'd feel as if she were playing a small part in what he was doing by turning the Rosalie over to him.

Anton was thinking of Teta Adelka as the three of them carried Tereza to the car, still draped in the blanket. His greatest fear was that they'd be caught, arrested, and the car would be traced back to his aunt, even though he'd put it in his name. He'd been seen driving her car in the past, before the invasion, on the rare occasion when he borrowed it or drove Teta Adelka somewhere. He figured it was better to continue using the Rosalie than to call attention to himself by buying a car, something he'd never done before.

Anton and Erik held Tereza while Jakub opened both back doors. They managed to slide her onto the backseat, and Anton perched on the edge. The others got into the front, with Jakub in the driver's seat. "Let's go to the barn first so you can help me carry her in. Then you can take Erik home. Come back to the barn, and we'll figure out how to get you home." Jakub was nineteen, and not to be trusted for any length of time with the Rosalie. Anton wondered at times whether he could be trusted with their work. He was courageous, but prone to taking unnecessary risks.

The abandoned farm was located at the end of the dirt road, near where it intersected with the highway. They drove down the lane and into the field beside the barn with lights off. Anton went into the barn with his flashlight and immediately heard rats squeaking. They were probably just as hungry as the humans who had abandoned the place. The floor was dirt with a little hay scattered around. There was no way they could take Tereza up the ladder to the hayloft, so he climbed up and threw down armloads of hay to make a bed for her. They carried her in and laid her on the hay.

"I can't leave her here alone," Anton said. "I hear rats, and with those open wounds—"

"I could take the car home and leave it in the alley by the apartment. I'll come back tomorrow, and we can work out something," Jakub said.

"No, Erik, you drive Jakub home. Then come back, and you can walk home from here. Jakub, call Dr. Havelka when you get there. You know his number. Go in with him, Erik, and make sure everything gets worked out before you come back. Give him exact instructions for finding this place. You can turn on the lights once you're on the highway, but leave them off on the dirt road. Let me get the parachute and the suit and helmet out of the back before you go. I'll bury them here beside the barn. It looks like whoever lived here had animals that trampled the dirt outside, so I don't think anyone will notice that I've been digging. Keep an eye on her and keep the rats away while I get rid of this stuff."

He dug a hole with a shovel that had been in Tereza's pack, buried the items and walked over the area to smooth it, and then went inside to check on Tereza as Erik drove off with Jakub. Her pulse was still steady; she moaned slightly and was still. He shined his flashlight on her face—she was beautiful, just as he'd been told, in spite of the scratches on the right side of her face. Her hair was a golden blonde that would help convince anyone she was Czech.

Flashing the light around them, he saw red eyes reflected back at him. Damn the rats. He couldn't leave her for a minute. It was a half hour to Prague, so Erik should be back in an hour. It was almost five, and the sky was beginning to get light in the East. Erik would be back by six. The barn had an opening large enough for a hay wagon, and he could drive the Rosalie in so it wouldn't be seen from the air. In the meantime, he'd leave the flashlight on so he could see what was creeping around in the corners.

#

He heard the car turn off the highway and onto the dirt road just after six. Both doors opened; Erik got out of the driver's

5

side and Dr. Havelka opened the passenger door. "His car's in the shop," Erik said. "I have to get home before my parents wake up, if they aren't up already. I'm leaving now to walk home."

"I explained to him that you can't leave her here," the doctor said. "The barn's too dirty, and with the rats, well, we have to take her to my place. I can take better care of her there. You can drive me, Anton, and help me get her settled. As you know, we have a place for her."

"What if we're stopped on the way?"

"We'll tell them she was injured when someone ran into her on her bicycle, like you discussed before. They'll believe me—I'm a doctor."

Anton had always admired Dr. Havelka's bravery while at the same time considering him somewhat naïve. He was a short, pudgy man who looked thoughtful in gold-rimmed glasses. "We'll leave her at your place for as short a time as possible. Then I'll move her to the apartment we've rented for her. I can stay with her there as much as necessary." Endangering the doctor was the last thing Anton wanted to do. He was too valuable; he had patched up two gunshot wounds during the time Anton had been active in the resistance. Now Tereza would present an even greater challenge.

Erik was still standing beside them as they stood over Tereza, as if waiting for Anton's permission to leave. "Go on home, Erik. I don't want you to have trouble leaving the next time we need you. Thanks for your help." They shook hands.

"Let me know when you need me." He turned and walked away.

Dr. Havelka had brought a makeshift stretcher that fit in the backseat of the car, and they moved Tereza onto it and carried her easily to the Rosalie. "Will she be okay back there by herself?" Anton asked.

"I'll reach back and hold her steady. The bleeding's virtually stopped. You fellows did a good job with that."

Anton's worst fear was that she was bleeding internally and that she'd die before they reached the doctor's office. "Do you think she has internal injuries?"

6

"I doubt she does, but we can tell more about her condition when I get her home." Dr. Havelka lived upstairs over his office with his wife Anna and assorted cats.

"I understand she's a nurse," Anton said. "Her expertise should be helpful in her recovery."

"That's a definite plus," the doctor said as they started toward Prague.

#

Dr. Havelka lived just a few blocks from Teta Adelka on Valdstejnska Street in Mala Strana, or Lesser Town, and Anton knew the area well. He drove into an alley behind the doctor's house. With any luck, they'd be able to transfer Tereza to the house before anyone was awake in the neighboring homes. They left the car doors open to keep from waking the neighbors, slid Tereza and the stretcher from the car, and took her into the house.

They lifted her off the stretcher and onto a hospital bed in a room at the back of the house, a room that contained only the bed with a light over it and a cabinet Anton assumed was full of medical supplies. "You must go home now and get some sleep," the doctor said. "Anna will come down and help me with her."

"I need to get the car out of the alley and out of sight. I'll walk back later and see how she's doing when I've had some sleep."

#

Anton's landlady had no car; it had disappeared years ago along with her husband, so she was happy to rent her tiny garage to him when he rented the apartment above her shop in Old Town. The garage was located at the back of her bakery and was so small that there was barely room for him to squeeze out of the Rosalie once the car was inside. At least the car was hidden, so it was worth the inconvenience. Rickety stairs led up the side of the building to his flat, and he could see that a light was on inside when he came around the building from the garage. He went back to the car and took his vz.22 from its hiding place under the dashboard.

He put the pistol in the waistband of his trousers and went back to the stairs. When he reached the top, he removed the gun with his right hand and tried the doorknob with his left. The door was unlocked. When he pushed it open, he could see through the small sitting area to the bedroom, and there, in his bed, was Eliska Muller.

She pulled the sheet up to her chin. "Don't shoot!" She was smiling.

He put the pistol in a box on his bookshelf. "What are you doing here?"

"You promised to take me to breakfast."

"That was yesterday. I took you to breakfast yesterday."

"I thought you were taking me again today. And every day. What are you doing with a gun?"

"I inherited it from my grandfather. I think he got it shortly after the war."

"The war?"

"The first World War."

"You know you're not supposed to own a gun now."

"It's an heirloom. I can't get rid of it. I keep it hidden."

"It wasn't hidden just now. You must have taken it somewhere." She kept looking at him, waiting for an explanation.

"I was visiting some friends in the country. We were target practicing. They just dropped me off. I saw the light was on, and I thought you might be a burglar."

"Why didn't you take me along to the country? Now that my divorce is underway, there's no problem with being seen together. I'd love to shoot a gun."

Eliska was spoiled, rich, and gorgeous. Her blonde hair cascaded over the pillow and she was looking at him with eyes the color of jade. In spite of his fatigue, he wanted her.

"Come to bed with me. I have absolutely nothing on under this sheet. We'll go to breakfast later."

He took off his clothes, dropped them on the floor, and slid under the sheet with her. Her skin was like satin as she moved against him, turning him on his back and touching him all over. This was Eliska: assertive—no, aggressive—in bed, and his fatigue was forgotten as he took her in his arms.

#

They both dozed afterward. He woke after a couple of hours and began wondering about her for the hundredth time. Their affair had begun before the war, when her German husband lived with her in Prague. She had come to him to make some inquiries about divorce. Nothing definite at the time, just inquiries. She wasn't happy with Kurt Muller, who was the son of a rich industrialist and a bit of a playboy. Anton wondered back then whether she would ever be truly content with any man, but he couldn't resist her advances, or maybe it was just that he didn't want to, and the affair began.

He thought she probably was seeing others, too, but it didn't really matter. He liked her, and admired her wit and intelligence, but the affair was all about sex. No love was involved on either side. His only worry now was that she was married to a German, and she didn't seem to have a strong reaction to what had happened to Czechoslovakia. Her feelings centered on her own happiness and on the people in her circle who could contribute to it.

Kurt Muller had turned out to be more patriot than playboy, and when Germany invaded Poland, he rushed home to Berlin to enlist. Now she had begun divorce proceedings in earnest, and Anton had turned her case over to a colleague, explaining to her that it would be best for someone else to handle it since they were involved.

She opened her eyes. "I'm hungry."

"I am, too. Let's go get something, and then you need to go home. I have things to do today." What he needed to do was get five or six more hours of sleep before walking back to Dr. Havelka's to check on Tereza.

Now she was pouting. "I wanted us to do something today."

"Sorry; I can't."

She got up and started putting on her bra, and he grabbed her and pulled her back into bed. She pushed him away. "Let me go! If you aren't going to spend the day with me, I'm not going back to bed with you."

"Okay, okay, let's get something to eat." He went to the bathroom. "I need a shower first."

She came to be bathroom door. "You've hardly been at your office at all lately. What are you up to? Not seeing another woman, I hope."

He knew she wouldn't care if he were seeing another woman. This was just her way of pretending he was her only paramour and that she wasn't the libertine he knew she was.

She must have been visiting his colleague, the one handling the divorce, the one who undoubtedly suspected what he was up to and covered for him. "Not all my business is conducted in the office. I have several elderly clients who insist on seeing me in their homes."

She said no more, and they went downstairs to Mrs. Svobodova's bakery where, because he was her renter and she liked him, she would fix them eggs to go with their pastries if she had any and wasn't busy. He couldn't shake the uneasy feeling that came over him when Eliska asked why he wasn't spending more time in his office. True, she was divorcing the German, but did she know others? And what was her relationship with them?

CHAPTER TWO

When Adelka Janakova heard the faintest of noises upstairs, she knew it couldn't be Zita, the maid. Zita had left just minutes before to go grocery shopping. She went to the bottom of the stairs and listened; she heard nothing more. But there had been something, she was sure of it, and she felt the need to check. If a rodent had gotten into the attic, she'd have to do something about it. She'd be able to hear better upstairs if that were the case. She'd ask Zita, whose room was on the second floor, whether she'd noticed anything.

She almost welcomed a reason to go upstairs, since she hadn't gone to the second floor lately. Her nephew, Anton Janak, had insisted that she move to a downstairs bedroom so she wouldn't have to climb the stairs. He had come with one of his partners, Josef Mares, and they had switched all the furniture between her upstairs bedroom and the one downstairs that she normally used for guests. Now that the war was on, people weren't visiting anyway, and she'd turn her former bedroom to a guest room after the war.

When she got to the second-floor hallway, she could see that the door to the last room on the right was closed. This was unusual, since Zita cleaned up here at least once a week and didn't bother closing the doors. Adelka felt the slightest hesitation about opening the door, but then what could be behind it? She and Zita were in the house all the time, so no one could have come in without their knowing it.

She turned the knob and pushed the door open. A young man who looked to be in his mid-twenties was sitting on the edge of the bed. "What are you doing in my house?" she asked.

"I needed a place to stay until arrangements can be made for me to leave Prague."

Zita must have had something to do with this. "And how did you happen to pick my house?"

"I know Zita."

His manner was straightforward enough. He must be a member of the resistance, but hadn't they been practically wiped out with all the reprisals after Heydrich's assassination? At least that was the word whispered among the older ladies in her church group. Then again there was the situation with Anton. He was involved in something clandestine, she was virtually sure of it, so there must be at least a rudimentary movement in place.

"You're wanted by someone, I suppose. What's your name?"

"Gustav."

"It's not the Prague police, is it?" She wasn't about to harbor a criminal.

"No, ma'am."

She'd really have to have a word with Zita for doing something like this without letting her know. These were strange times, however, and she couldn't help feeling elated about doing something against the SS or Gestapo, any small effort to repay them for Cyril's death. She was his older sister, she'd always been protective of him, and this might be her chance to start getting even. She believed the young man when he said the police weren't looking for him, and she wouldn't ask anything more, at least not now.

"You may stay here until you're able to leave. Do you have any ration stamps?"

"No, and no money. I had to leave everything behind."

"We'll manage." Somehow, Zita found enough food, and that was something else that Adelka wondered about but didn't ask. The black market was rampant throughout the city, this much she knew. She and Zita were able to eat, and to feed Anton when he came to take her somewhere. Now they'd feed Gustav, too.

#

Adelka poured soup into a bowl, added a spoon, and started up the stairs with it. Zita usually took lunch to the young man in the spare bedroom, but she was out shopping for food again.

12

When Adelka had confronted Zita about Gustav, she said he was a friend who was out of work and needed a place to stay until he found a job. Adelka knew there was more to the story, since Gustav indicated he needed to get out of Prague, and when he hadn't left the house or even the upstairs during the first week, she sat Zita down and insisted she tell the truth about her friend.

Zita's pretty face looked troubled. "I know how you feel about the Nazis, so I hoped you wouldn't mind. He's on the run from them. He was involved in a clandestine operation—I'm not sure what it was, and he wouldn't tell me. Anyway, he'll be sent to another area soon. I appreciate your helping him. We went to school together."

Adelka wondered why she felt like laughing, when she needed to scold Zita. "You should have told me the truth from the beginning. Then I could have had the opportunity to decide whether our safety was more important than helping him. However, it's done now, he's here, and he can stay till he can leave safely. You've done a marvelous job getting food for us, so I've no doubt you'll be able to get enough so that we can continue feeding him, too." She felt like hugging the girl, not just for her skill in furnishing food, but also for providing the opportunity to strike at the Nazis.

What would Anton think if he knew what she was involved in? It wouldn't do to tell him now, but after the war, she would. They both could laugh about it then. And he probably had stories of his own to share. She was virtually sure he was involved with the resistance, or what was left of it, but he would be even more concerned about her than she was about him if he knew about the mysterious stranger in the upper bedroom. She prayed for Anton every night, and she didn't know what else to do to alleviate her worries about him.

His mother had died when he was six, and shortly after his father took a position in the law school at Charles University. They moved in with her; Anton stayed till he was ready to start law school, and Cyril continued living with her until his death of a heart attack on the night the invasion began. Now she had an opportunity to strike back at the Nazis; she would do everything in her power to see that the young man was safe as long as he was in her household.

CHAPTER THREE

It wasn't that far from Old Town, where Anton's flat was located, to Valdstejnska Street in the stately residential area where Teta Adelka and Dr. Havelka lived. It was a brilliant September afternoon, and he was enjoying the walk. He crossed the Vltava and walked by his old apartment building. He still regretted giving up the place, since it was one of the nicest in town, with a fine view of the city. He had felt, when he became involved in the resistance, that a less conspicuous place would be better, especially one with a hiding place for the Rosalie. And he was saving enough on rent to almost make up for his losses at the law office.

This was something else Eliska questioned, his change of apartments, but he told her he'd always wanted to live in Old Town, to get to know every street and alleyway there. And this wasn't entirely untrue. He was enjoying his time there, and his apartment, through small, was comfortable. There was a tiny sitting area with an alcove for a kitchen, a bedroom with a firm bed, which was to his liking, and a bath.

He approached the doctor's office from the alley at the rear and went in the back entrance. The door to the room where Tereza was being kept was closed, and he tapped lightly. Dr. Havelka's wife Anna opened the door. "Come in. We've been expecting you. I was just changing dressings. We managed to cut off her clothes and get her into a gown."

"Can I help?" How he could help, he couldn't imagine, but he felt he should ask.

"No, I'm through now. Tomas is seeing patients in the front, but he'll be back in a little while to check on her. Sit down if you want to wait and talk to him."

15

A chair had been moved into the room, and Anton sat down. "I'll wait for him. I need to find out how long her recovery's going to take."

Anna left, and he looked at Tereza. She was sleeping peacefully, her chest rising and falling lightly under a white sheet. Or maybe this couldn't be considered sleep, but a coma, or unconsciousness. Again he questioned the wisdom of sending a woman on such a mission. However, the fact that she was a real beauty might make getting information from the SS easier.

He thought about the message he would have to compose and translate into code. "Package received damaged. Delivery system failed. Repairs may take . . ." the doctor would supply this information. "Please advise if postponement is possible."

Dr. Havelka came in, looking as if he'd had a long day. After all, he'd had a pre-dawn trip to a barn in the country before his usual workday started. "She's doing remarkably well. I had to put a cast on her left leg, and I sewed up the lacerations. She has a knot on the side of her head and a concussion, in spite of the helmet she was wearing. We're checking on her frequently."

"She hasn't opened her eyes yet?"

"No, but I'm hoping that will happen soon."

"Do you have any idea when she'll be able to get around town, walking or riding a bicycle?"

"If everything goes well, it should take six to eight weeks. The main thing now is to let her rest and let the leg heal."

"Is there anything I can do here?"

"No, we have everything under control. You look like you could use a good night's sleep."

Anton took a slip of paper from his pocket. "I want you to have my phone number, in case you need to get in touch with me. It would be best if you memorize it and burn this." He had been warned not to give out his number, but circumstances had changed, and some decisions had to be made on the spur of the moment.

Dr. Havelka nodded. Anton had no doubt he would do exactly as requested. "I'll go then. I have more work to do tonight, and then I will get a good night's sleep."

He walked home as twilight settled over the city. It was his favorite time of day, but tonight the Germans were out in force in the bars and restaurants as he made his way through Old Town. He was wearing a pair of shabby trousers and a faded shirt, both items borrowed from Erik, in an attempt to look like a workingman making his way home from the job. A German officer approached with a young Czech girl on his arm. He murmured something to the girl, and they both looked at Anton and laughed. He looked straight ahead and kept walking, grateful when he reached the sanctuary of his apartment.

What day was it? Was this some sort of German holiday, or were they simply taking advantage of a beautiful evening? The drop had been scheduled for Wednesday, so this was still Wednesday. It seemed like a week had passed since he stood and watched helplessly as Tereza's parachute fluttered downward. He couldn't let himself get so tired that he wasn't thinking clearly, that he wasn't even sure what day it was.

He warmed the thin soup his landlady had brought him just before he left the flat and ate it with two chunks of bread he had put away for an evening such as this. He washed the warming pot he had eaten from and the spoon, and then dried them and put them away. He went to the bookcase and took down a book of Kafka short stories and began coding the message.

When he was done, he burned the original in the sink and washed the ashes down the drain. He went to the phone, dialed, and let it ring twice. Tyn Church, tomorrow, ten a.m. His phone rang once—message received. Now if Eliska would stay away tonight, maybe he could get a full night's sleep. He took a shower, set the alarm for nine a.m., and went to bed.

#

The tapping at his door was so light, he was sure it wasn't the Germans coming for him. He picked up the clock and took it to the window, where the sky full of stars was casting a faint light. Three-seventeen a.m. The tapping began again. He went to the door and opened it a crack. Erik was standing there, looking as if he were trying to shrink into the side of the building. He was dressed in black.

17

"What the devil are you doing here?" Anton whispered. He grabbed Erik's shirt and dragged the gangly teenager into the flat. "I told you not to come to my apartment, and coming at night is the worst thing you could do. There's the curfew to think about, and everything looks more suspicious to the Nazis when it's dark."

"I know, but I couldn't get away during the day. My parents would have noticed, and they would have wanted an explanation."

"What's happened?"

"The Germans came to the field today. Two carloads of them. I was working in our field that's next to the one where Tereza landed. I heard cars on the dirt road. I walked back through the trees, and I could see them. One of them climbed the tree."

"Were they Gestapo, or SS?" What difference did it make?

"I couldn't be sure, but I didn't want to take a chance on getting any closer."

"No, you were right. It doesn't matter anyway. They must have noticed the tree from the air. Or maybe that plane we heard did see our torches before we put them out." What were the chances that he had left a shred of the parachute or its cords in the tree, working in darkness with a flashlight? And even if he had found it all, they would have searched the woods and found the torches.

"I didn't want to come to town at night, but I thought you should know."

"Did you walk all the way?"

"No. A farmer was making deliveries to restaurants on the edge of town. He has some kind of special permit."

"Yes, the Germans like the restaurants to be well supplied for their eating pleasure."

"He dropped me off a couple of miles from here, and I walked the rest of the way."

"You'll have to stay here till morning. You can leave when the streets are full of people going to work. We can't take a chance on your being stopped."

Erik nodded. "I know it's the smart thing to do. But God, my parents are going to be frantic. They suspect already that I'm involved in something, and they're terrified."

"You need to invent a girlfriend."

"They'd be almost as upset if they thought I spent the night out with a girlfriend."

Anton was so tired he couldn't think of a way to placate the parents. They'd just have to be worried. Some parents would be cheering their son on, probably even joining in his clandestine efforts. Not the case here and never would be, and he couldn't think of anything right now to do about it.

"Let's have a glass of wine. I have a little I've been saving, and maybe it'll help us sleep." He took down the bottle from the top shelf of the kitchen cabinet and poured what little was left into two water glasses. It was ice wine he bought in Mikulov just before the invasion. "You can sleep on the couch . . . you did the right thing, coming to tell me. It's just that it would have been better if you had come during the day." Life would be less complicated if Erik's family had a phone.

They drank their wine in silence. Anton gave Erik an extra pillow and saw that his lanky body was squeezed onto the couch, and then went to bed himself. The wine was no help at all. There was too much to think about. The Germans knew that there had been a parachute drop, and that someone had landed in the tree. They'd assume that person had been injured if they weren't killed, so they'd be searching every medical facility in the area. They'd undoubtedly start with the hospitals and move on to all the doctor's offices in town. Tereza would have to be moved, but moving her was doubly risky now.

The doctor's car had a trunk. It wasn't a pleasant thought, but maybe they could haul her in the trunk to the flat they had rented for her. The doctor had reasons to be on the streets at night, so he could visit her at the apartment when necessary. Anton knew he would have to stay with her for a while, and Mrs. Svobodova might get suspicious if he stayed away from the flat for a long period of time. And what would the landlady do if she were suspicious? Maybe nothing. At least he hoped so.

19

He heard the door open and close at five, and he jumped up and ran to look out. Erik was just disappearing around the corner, and Anton knew he couldn't create the commotion of chasing after him. Damn these kids! Why was he saddled with teenagers? And now a woman. There was nothing to be done but hope Erik would make it home without being caught and Tereza could be moved with no problems.

He finally dozed, and the alarm sounded at nine. He dressed in the same workingman's clothes he wore the day before and went downstairs to the bakery. Mrs. Svobodova had found coffee somewhere, and she poured a cup for him. She had a piece of bread also, and a small sweet roll she brought up from under the counter. She told him she had potatoes and would make soup later in the day, so he paid her for that, too, when he left.

The church was a short walk, and he arrived there a few minutes before ten. The hushed atmosphere always gave Anton a feeling of tranquility, at least for the short time he was there. He walked down the center aisle and sat in a pew near the front. He was alone in the church; he took the coded message from inside his shirt and slipped it into a newspaper he picked up along the way.

The tall, thin man who met him faithfully each time he called sat down beside him. "Good morning. Anything interesting in the paper today?"

"Just the usual." His contact would know the paper was full of the usual Nazi propaganda. Anton's thoughts now were on getting to the doctor's office and solving the problem of getting Tereza out of there. "I've finished reading. Would you like the paper?"

"Yes, thanks." The contact looked around. "I feel the need to give you an early warning. There's been talk that something needs to be done about the Skoda Munitions Works. I—"

"By something, you mean sabotage, or a fire . . . something like that?"

"Nothing has been decided yet, but the thinking is that the production of panzers needs to be slowed down or stopped. It's almost certain you'll be involved, whatever is decided."

20

Anton nodded. Here was something more to worry about. But he had more pressing problems at the moment, and he stood up to leave. "Thanks for letting me know. I must go now."

The contact picked up the paper and began looking at the headlines. Anton nodded at the man and left. From the church he walked to Dr. Havelka's office, again entering through the back. He tapped on the door to the room where Tereza was being kept and got no answer. He went in; she was lying just as she was when he was there last. If he waited here long enough, someone would come to check on her.

It wasn't long till Dr. Havelka came in. "I don't know what's going on, but an acquaintance of mine, a doctor, called me earlier. He said the Gestapo came and searched his office from top to bottom. He was going to call all the doctors he knows to warn them. I've been calling some myself. Do you know what's happening? More importantly, we need to do something with Tereza immediately."

"The Nazis went to the field where she landed. They know someone came down in the tree, and of course they assume that person was injured. Is your car here?"

"They brought it back this morning. It's in the garage."

"Let's put her in the trunk and drive her somewhere. Tell the patients in the waiting room you've been called away on an emergency."

"I can't leave Anna here alone to face the Gestapo. You take the car and take her somewhere in the country. Do you have any relatives who could help?"

"My only relative nearby is an aunt, who lives just down the street."

"Could you take her there?"

"The biggest problem with that is she has a maid that I'm not sure of. She's fairly new, and I don't know her that well."

"Might be risky. Take her back to that barn, drive the car into the barn, and get her into the front of the car. Don't take her out of the car. Remember the rats."

"I could drive back into town after dark. Let me have your permit. Maybe I'll take her to my apartment." As soon as he said this, he knew it wouldn't work. He wasn't thinking clearly. What if Eliska came by and found her there? It would be more than a problem, it could be a disaster. And the landlady usually brought food every day. What would she think if she saw a young woman with a cast on her leg? He'd have to take her to the apartment they rented for her a few blocks from his.

Anton was impressed with the way Dr. Havelka gave up his permit without hesitation. Would that there were more like him. They went to Tereza's room and put her on the stretcher. Anton could see they had found a dress for her somewhere, and she had a shoe and sock on her right foot that looked as if they came off the foot of a farm worker. They carried her to the garage without looking around to see who was watching. It would be best to act as if they were performing an everyday task, that it didn't matter if anyone was watching or not. Once inside the garage, they shut the door and lifted her into the trunk.

Anton drove out, wondering about the air supply in the trunk. Surely it was ample for the half-hour drive to the barn. He hoped the Nazis would be so busy searching medical facilities that they wouldn't be setting up roadblocks. He was afraid to speed—the worst thing he could do would be to call attention to himself.

When he reached the barn, he drove inside far enough, he hoped, so that the car couldn't be seen from the dirt road. He got out quickly and opened the trunk to find a wide-awake Tereza staring at him.

CHAPTER FOUR

The man was looking at her as if he were surprised to find her in his trunk. "Where am I?" She said the words in English and then had the feeling that she shouldn't be speaking English. She wasn't sure why, but nothing was clear at this point.

"You're okay, but no English, please." He was speaking Czech and smiling now, so he seemed less formidable.

"Where am I," this time in Czech.

"You're in the trunk of a Rolls Royce in a barn in the Czech countryside. I need to carry you to the front of the car, and then we can talk." He picked her up, and a pain shot through her left leg that was sharp enough to make her gasp. "Sorry." He placed her on the passenger seat, then went around and got in behind the wheel.

She was concerned about saying anything until she could figure out what was happening to her, so she waited for him to speak.

"Do you remember parachuting into Czechoslovakia?"

"No." She would say as little as possible till she decided whether she could trust this man.

"Your chute didn't open—well, it partially opened at the last minute, and you managed somehow to land in a tree. Or maybe a gust of wind just blew you there. Anyway, that was Wednesday at about two a.m. We took you to the office of a doctor in Prague, and he sewed up your cuts and put a cast on your leg. Then the Nazis came to the field where you landed and were snooping around, so we knew they'd be searching the medical facilities for an injured jumper. I had to bring you here. Do you remember your name?"

"I'm Alexandra Novak." She saw him cringe when she said this and thought it was a reaction to the fact that she didn't use Novakova, putting the traditional Czech feminine ending on

23

her surname. But then, it just wasn't done in America. He surely could understand that.

"No, you're Tereza Valentova. You must never say the other name again. Do you remember why you're here?"

The fog in her mind was beginning to lift a little. "I'm Tereza Valentova from the Sudetenland. My father was Czech and my mother German, which explains why I speak both languages." She found herself saying the words as if they had been imprinted on her brain. She wondered why she was saying them, when she knew she was Alexandra Novak. "What day is it now?"

"It's Thursday. It was only yesterday morning that you arrived."

"Why didn't my parachute open?"

"There was no way of telling. It was tangled in the tree, and I had to rip it and cut it to get it out of the tree. Of course, we had to bury it immediately, so we'll never know what happened. Maybe it wasn't packed properly."

She wanted to curl up in the backseat and sleep, but it seemed like too much trouble to get back there with the cast on her leg. "My leg hurts."

"The doctor gave me some pills for the pain and a jar of water. I'll get them." He got out and opened the trunk, and then returned and took the lid off a glass jar. "You'll have to drink out of the jar. I don't have anything else." He handed her a small white pill.

She still wasn't sure she trusted him, but she was desperate to take something for the pain, so she swallowed the pill. "My head hurts, too."

"I hope the pill will fix it. Do you remember why you came here?"

"Everything seems a jumble right now." Actually, she was beginning to remember a lot of things, but she didn't know how much she should divulge. The man beside her probably wanted her to think he was Czech, but he didn't look like the Czech descendants she knew back in Texas. They all had blonde hair and green eyes like she did. Maybe she should ask, but would he tell her the truth? Maybe he was a Nazi trying to get information from her, but he didn't look like a German, either. "Are you Czech?"

"Yes, I was born here."

"You don't look much like the Czechs I know."

"There are plenty of Czechs who don't really look like Czechs. My great-grandmother was Romanian. Her hair was dark, too. Actually, I've always suspected she was a gypsy, but no one in the family wants to talk about it. Especially now, when the Nazis are rounding up gypsies and other groups they consider undesirable. Everyone else in my family has blonde hair, but I took after her."

His eyes were gray, and his skin was fair. One thing she didn't want to do at this point was to assess his attractiveness, but it was difficult not to notice that he was extremely attractive. Obviously he was trying to keep the conversation light, hoping she would trust him. "What's our next move?"

"We have to wait here till well after dark. Then I'll take you to an apartment we rented for you. You'll have to stay there till you're well enough to continue with the work you were sent here to do."

"What about food? And I have a feeling I don't have any clothes other than what I'm wearing."

"I'll take care of things. Unfortunately, food isn't plentiful here, but we'll do the best we can. I have a landlady who owns a bakery that the Nazis enjoy, so she's able to get things the average shop owner doesn't have access to."

Tereza heard a noise behind the car, and she turned to see a huge man walking toward the car with a pitchfork in his hand.

CHAPTER FIVE

Anton turned toward the back of the car and saw the man approaching. He thought about his gun in the box on his bookshelf and wished he'd remembered to put it back in the car. He'd never killed anyone, but this might have been his first experience if he had the gun, because the hulking man approaching them was carrying a pitchfork. If he didn't harm them, he might memorize their license plate and describe the car to the Nazis, which would put the doctor in jeopardy. As it was, without the gun, he'd have to bluff. The car windows were down, and it was too late to roll all of them up. He put his hand on Tereza's leg; she jerked away at first and then seemed to understand.

"What are you doing in my barn?" He was standing beside Anton's door.

Anton smiled and hoped the smile was convincing. "Just looking for a little privacy. My wife has spies all over town, so my girlfriend and I look for a place in the country. You look like a married man. You know what wives can be like."

The man stood there pondering this for a moment. He looked directly at Tereza. "You get out of the car." Then at Anton. "You get out of here."

Anton opened the door with all the force he could muster in such a confined space, slamming it into the man and knocking him down. He shut the door and started the car, but the man hoisted himself up on the side of the car and then reached in and cut off the engine. "Get out," he shouted at Tereza. He had dropped his pitchfork when he fell, and he now reached through the window and began choking Anton. Anton punched him in the stomach, but this was like punching a bag of cement. He tried unsuccessfully to pry the man's fingers

27

from around his throat. Then his attacker gasped and slowly sank to the ground.

Tereza was standing beside the man with the pitchfork in her hands. How in the devil had she managed to get out of the car and around to the other side with the cast on her leg? He gasped and caught his breath. "Thank you."

"Don't mention it. You'd better drag him to the back of the barn and get us out of here." Her face was white. She dropped the pitchfork and hobbled back to the passenger side.

"I'll help you get back in the car. Then I'll get rid of Attila the Hun here." He sounded more flippant than he felt; the episode had left him shaken. He'd been trained in killing by the resistance, but he'd never seen a man die in front of him. For a moment he thought he was going to be sick, but he managed to control the feeling.

He noticed that Tereza was shaking as she stood there staring at the man. Anton helped her into the passenger seat, then knelt by the man and felt for a pulse. There was none. He could see blood oozing from his side. It took all his strength to drag the body to the back of the barn, where he placed it beside some bales of hay. He placed the pitchfork, tines down, next to the body after wiping it down with his handkerchief. Maybe whoever discovered him would think he fell on the pitchfork.

He started the car. "We need to get out of here before anyone else shows up." They reached the highway and he turned west, away from Prague. "I'll stop somewhere and see if I can find something to eat. I can't take you in anywhere with the Nazis looking for an injured person, but I'll get something and bring it to the car. Are you hungry?"

"I'm starving. I guess that's a healthy sign."

"We need to get you some crutches. The doctor has some, but in our rush to get you out of his office we forgot to put them in the car. We weren't thinking about them because we didn't know when you'd wake up and be able to use them. We'll get you settled in the apartment tonight, and I'll return the doctor's car. Maybe he can drive me back to the apartment with the crutches. I can't take a chance on being seen with them on the street."

They came to Hostivice, where they spotted a small store beside the road. The proprietor looked out the window as Anton walked in; he was taking an interest in the Rolls Royce. "May I help you?"

The shelves were nearly bare. "I'd like some food. Do you have anything?"

"Do you have coupons?"

Anton took his ration card from his pocket. He had given most of the coupons to Mrs. Svobodova for the food she furnished him.

"I have a little bread and cheese. Also a couple of apples." He obviously had seen that there was another person in the car.

"I'll take all that." He'd give it to Tereza. Mrs. Svobodova had mentioned that she was making something—potato soup, wasn't it? He'd have that later—exactly when, he wasn't sure. He paid and gave what was left of his ration cards to the shopkeeper.

He insisted he wasn't hungry, so Tereza devoured the bread and cheese as he drove down the highway. She said he had to at least have one of the apples. He found another dirt road that led down to a small creek where two boys were fishing. Anton took the apples from the brown paper bag the clerk had given him and hoped the boys would go home soon, but they were fascinated with the Rolls Royce. They soon abandoned their poles and came to stare at the car.

"Is that your car, mister?" the older one asked.

"It belongs to my boss. He let me borrow it for today."

"What you doing down here by the creek?"

"We came down to eat our apples. Would you and your brother like part of one?"

"He ain't my brother, but he'd like some. I would, too."

Anton took a penknife from his pocket and cut his apple into thirds. Tereza tried to give him hers, but he insisted she eat it. He handed the kids their share.

"What happened to your leg, lady?"

Anton answered, establishing the alibi they originally thought of. "She was riding her bicycle and a car hit her. It broke her leg." The kids were going to go home and tell their families about seeing a Rolls Royce and a woman with a broken leg. They'd have to leave as soon as they finished the apples.

He started the car while the boys were still inspecting it. "Give us a ride!" the younger one shouted.

"Can't do it. Your fishing poles are going to get the seats wet and dirty."

"We'll leave them here. We come back every day."

Anton looked at Tereza and shrugged. He wondered whether she grasped their need for secrecy. "I'll give you a ride to the highway. You'll have to walk from there."

Now the older boy joined in. "To my house, please. I want my older brother to see me in a Rolls."

"Sorry, I can't do that. If you want a ride to the highway, get in."

They both climbed into the backseat and leaned back against the soft leather upholstery. "I'm going to tell my brother about this, but he'll never believe me."

Anton stopped at the highway, and the kids got out. "Thanks! Goodbye!" as the car disappeared.

"This isn't our day for being discreet," Anton said, glancing at Tereza.

She nodded as if she understood, then leaned against the seat and closed her eyes. The pain pill was making her sleepy.

He kept driving, hoping to find another side road where they could park in peace till dark. A paved road veered off from the highway they were on, and he decided to take it. Farther on, an unpaved road led to the right. Maybe it would take them to someone's home, or maybe to another creek where they'd find more people fishing.

The road was short, and it ended at a small farmhouse that had been abandoned. Those who had the opportunity were getting as far away from Prague as possible, it seemed. What would he do if someone showed up? He'd pretend to be a rich businessman who was considering buying the place as a weekend retreat. Even if the owner arrived, he could say they were out driving around in the country, looking for property that might be available.

He parked under a beech tree a short distance from the house. Tereza was sleeping soundly now. He should move to the backseat so he could put her leg up, but he decided not to wake her at the moment. He'd get out and roam around to see if he could find anything edible growing near the house. Mrs. Svobodova would be ecstatic if he found food.

Someone had planted a garden beside the house, but it looked as if it had been thoroughly harvested. Undoubtedly the property owners had taken everything with them when they left. The doors and windows were boarded up, so there was no possibility of checking the inside of the house. That would be useless anyway; since the garden had been picked clean, the house would have, too.

He returned to the car, wishing he had something to read. Tereza was awake. "I need to put my leg up. It's beginning to throb in spite of the pain pill."

He got out and lifted her injured leg to the seat as gently as possible. Maybe this would be a good time to see how much she remembered. He got into the backseat and sat in the corner opposite Tereza, facing her.

He wasn't sure she trusted him. If he had met her at the field when she descended from the sky, there would have been no question of his identity. Waking up in the trunk of a car to face a stranger who was now driving her all over the countryside probably didn't inspire much confidence. He couldn't think what he could do to make sure she accepted him as a member of the resistance. Maybe a few questions, and if she wouldn't answer, or couldn't, he could supply the facts that would convince her he was on her side. One thing she had going for her, her Czech was good. She sounded as if she could have come from the Sudetenland. And she had saved his life—something that Erik or Jakub might not have been able to accomplish. Maybe working with this particular woman wouldn't be so bad after all.

"Do you remember why you're in Czechoslovakia?"

She looked at him for a few seconds before answering. "I can't remember."

"You're here to work at the Cernin Palace in the Prague Castle area, which is now SS headquarters. You're to

31

photograph everything you can that would provide information about their plans for expanding the war, or any information that might be useful to the allies. You'll be a member of the cleaning crew."

"How can I get a job there? Do they just hire people off the street?"

"It will be arranged. How, I'm not sure. I don't need to know that, and they haven't told me. I take it you were recruited by the OSS."

She shrugged.

"I've been in touch with them, or with whomever it is you work for, to let them know about the accident. I've asked whether your mission can be postponed till you've recovered. When I can get back to my apartment I hope to get an answer. How is it that you speak both Czech and German, as well as English?"

"My grandparents on my father's side are natives of Czechoslovakia. My mother's parents are from Germany. We all live in the Schulenburg area, in Texas. I spent summers with both sets of grandparents since I was a toddler, since both my parents work. Neither of my grandmothers speaks much English, so I had to learn their languages."

"Texas. Land of cowboys and lots of cattle, right? Range wars and all that sort of thing. I love those movies."

Tereza smiled. "Texas is a lot more than that."

He hoped she wasn't going to be homesick. "You understand of course that here in Czechoslovakia, you're from the Sudetenland. It's a mountainous area on the German border, and a lot of people of German descent live there. Actually, it's part of Germany now. Your father was Czech and your mother German. Your parents owned an inn in the mountains near the town of Sokolov. They died in a fire when the inn burned. You came to Prague before the occupation to look for work as a translator. You worked in a small office for a while, but they went out of business when the Nazis came. Now all you could find was the cleaning job at the palace."

"Will the Germans check my background?"

"I'm sure they will. Everything's been arranged so that you'll appear to be who you say you are. I believe you came with a camera, ration cards, passport, etc. Those were in the jump suit you were wearing when you arrived. We weren't sure you were going to live, so we weren't too concerned about the items. Now they're of great importance. The doctor is saving these things for us, and when I return his car tonight, he'll give the stuff to me along with crutches. I'll get all this back to your apartment somehow. Do you remember how to use the camera?"

"Yes, I remember."

Maybe she was beginning to trust him. He had asked her about everything he had been told about her assignment and couldn't think of anything more. Then she surprised him by asking, "What sort of work do you do?"

"I'm an attorney. An attorney who isn't taking care of business lately. I'll have to go to my office tomorrow and spend some time. It's important that I keep up the façade of having a legitimate career."

"Do you practice alone?"

"I have three partners. We were in law school together. We're friends, and I think they've figured out what I'm involved in. At least one of them has. He's my best friend, and he's covering for me admirably. My main aim right now is to avoid endangering my partners, or anyone else I know. What sort of work did you do? I assume you were in the military when you were recruited by the OSS."

"I'm a nurse. An army nurse." She shifted her position as if to ease the pain in her leg. "Do you have relatives here?"

"An aunt. I'm especially concerned about her, and also my landlady, who's elderly. If either of them were taken in for questioning, it would destroy me. Probably more so than them. They're both strong women." He couldn't help thinking about how strong Tereza was, also. She had saved his life with a pitchfork in that barn. She was strong and attractive. But this wasn't the time to think about her attractiveness. Such thinking would be distracting, and he didn't need any distractions right now.

Still, it was inevitable that he'd compare her to Eliska—self-centered, sexy, witty Eliska, who would never be caught giving all for a cause. At least he could hope she wasn't devoted to helping the Germans, either. He was pretty sure such devotion was not in her makeup. His fear was that there were Germans in her circle of friends, and that she might inadvertently divulge something useful to them.

She had been insisting lately that they go out more together, now that her divorce was underway in earnest. She went to dinners and parties, and wanted him to go with her. He was the best-looking man she knew, she told him, and she wanted him beside her in his tuxedo, which she had spotted while snooping in his closet. Maybe it would be a good idea to go and check out her friends.

Tereza was dozing again, leaning against the door of the car. The sun had gone down, and twilight was spreading softly over the little farm. A thrush was singing itself to sleep in the tree overhead. He almost wished he owned the place, a retreat for when things got so bad in town he couldn't stand them any more. He could hide Tereza here if the situation ever got overly dangerous for her. This was ridiculous thinking, he told himself. He knew what the inevitable would be if the situation got truly dangerous for either of them.

He'd have to wake her. Would it be better to let her ride in the backseat, with her leg up, or in the front? The front would make more sense, in case they were stopped. The darkness might hide the fact that she had a cast on her leg. He touched her arm. "We have to leave now. I need to put your leg down."

She didn't complain as he moved her leg and turned her in the seat. He started the car and drove back to the highway with the lights off. All went well till they reached the edge of the city. He could see a roadblock ahead. He took the doctor's pass from his pocket. "Let me do the talking. My German is limited, and that may work in our favor. Cover your cast with your dress as much as you can."

They moved ahead in line till it was their turn. Soldiers came to either side of the car, and they rolled down the windows. Anton handed the man on his side the pass, and he looked it over. "Dr. Havelka. Where have you been?"

Anton understood this much. "In the country for an emergency. A child was injured when he fell from a tree." He wished the soldier hadn't mentioned Dr. Havelka's name. Tereza had no need to know that.

"The woman?"

"My nurse." Tereza must be smiling at the soldier on her side, because he was staring at her like a lovesick sheep. The man on his side of the car shined a flashlight over the interior. Anton resisted looking at Tereza's leg to see if the cast was showing.

"Move on! Next!"

His hands were shaking as he drove away. "Damn!" was all he could say.

"That was close."

"We'll be okay now," he said, sounding more confident than he felt. "You did great. Your dress must have covered the cast, and you seemed to have the man on your side entranced."

"A smile and a few flutters of the eyelashes can work wonders, it appears. I didn't know what else to do."

They arrived at her apartment without any more problems. The place had only one entrance. It was a basement apartment in an old building that had once held offices and now provided living quarters for the working class. "We have no choice but to park in front of the apartment and walk in," Anton said. Fortunately, the street was quiet.

He helped Tereza from the car. "If anyone comes along, we'll pretend we had too much to drink." He placed her arm around his neck, but maneuvering her from the car toward the steps was awkward. He picked her up gingerly, moving her leg as little as possible, and carried her to the stairs and down to the door. She was heavier than he imagined she would be, and carrying her was more pleasant than he imagined it would be, too, with her arm draped around his neck. He ignored an impulse to kiss her, reminding himself again that he had more than enough distractions.

They made it down the cement steps and to her door without seeing anyone. "I have keys here somewhere. They gave me two." He had both of them in his pocket since she arrived, and he took one out now and opened the door.

The apartment consisted of one large room with a single bed in one corner and a chest nearby, a couch, some cabinets, a counter with a hotplate, a sink, and a kitchen table with three mismatched chairs. Away from the street side a door opened into a bathroom. There was no closet. Just seeing it again made him feel that his place was luxurious. He helped her to the bathroom, where he could hear water running for quite a while.

She opened the door, and he helped her to the bed. "I need to take the car back to the doctor's garage and arrange to get crutches and supplies to you. I'll keep the spare key so you won't have to get up to let me in. You shouldn't answer knocks at the door, anyway. I'm going to put you to bed with another pain pill. I'll see if the doctor and his wife have any food I can bring."

"I'm not hungry right now. Just another pain pill and some sleep, that's what I want."

He gave her a pill and put the water jar on the chest. He looked in the drawers, and all were empty. They'd have to figure out a way to get her some clothes. Maybe Anna could help. She'd need something for going to work, or possibly they furnished uniforms. Something else to find out.

He locked the door and put the key back in his pocket. By the time he arrived at Dr. Havelka's, it was almost nine. He was opening the garage door when the doctor came outside. He was carrying crutches and a knapsack. "I've been watching for you. Close the garage door, and I'll take you where you need to go."

"That would be a tremendous help. It's just that I hate to put you in any more danger than you're already in."

"Like you, I'm in this all the way. I'll put these things in the trunk. Anna managed to get a few items of clothing at a secondhand store. They're in the knapsack along with Tereza's documents and the camera. How did she do today?"

"Pretty well, considering. She was awake when I opened the trunk to take her out, which was quite a surprise. I gave her a pain pill when we finally found a place to wait in the country, and I gave her another when I put her to bed at her apartment. I've been wondering about you and Anna all day. Did the Nazis show up and search your office?"

"They searched not only the office, but our upstairs apartment as well. It was thorough, but fortunately they were searching for a person and not that person's documents. I put those and the camera in my pocket, and Anna put the clothes she got for Tereza into the bureau drawers with hers. It was a tremendous relief when they finally left."

"Thank God they didn't find anything. I'm grateful for all you do." Anton gave the doctor back his permit and directed him to Tereza's apartment. "Take off as soon as I get the things out of the trunk. I'll walk to my place from here."

"It's late. I can wait and drive you."

"No. You must get on home. I'll see how Tereza's doing, and I may stay with her for a while to make sure she's okay. I'll be fine."

The doctor stopped at the curb and Anton took the things from the trunk and hurried down the stairs to the apartment. Tereza was awake when he let himself in. "I brought you some crutches, and all the items that were in your jump suit are now in this knapsack. All but the small shovel, that is. I used it to bury the parachute and your jumpsuit, and then I covered it with dirt. The doctor's wife found some more clothes for you, and they're in there, too. Will you be okay here if I go to my place for a while?"

"I'll be fine. Just leave the crutches beside the bed, in case I need to get up. I don't think it's safe for you to be out, however. Isn't there a curfew?"

Anton laughed. "I don't know what the word safe means now. You won't either after you recover and get involved. I'll be back later and spend the rest of the night here. I can sleep on the couch. And yes, there is a curfew."

"Please be careful."

Was she actually concerned about him, or was she concerned about what would happen to her if he were caught and detained. He preferred to think it was the first, while at the same time reminding himself that this kind of thinking was irrelevant. "I'll be careful, and I'll be back." He took a side street to a less popular thoroughfare then made his way to the alley behind his apartment. All was quiet.

He opened his door and saw that the landlady had left the promised potato soup by his stove. Did he dare carry it back to Tereza's? He certainly couldn't carry it in the pot, and he had nothing to put it in that would be less conspicuous. He was famished, and she had said earlier she wasn't hungry, so he started warming it while he made the first phone call. He let it ring once, hung up and waited a minute, then dialed and let it ring once again. He heard an answering two rings. His contact had a reply to his message and would meet him tomorrow afternoon at three at the Café Slavia.

He ate the soup and washed up, showered and dressed in pajamas, then put on a suit and clean white shirt over them. He couldn't sleep in his suit, so this might work. He'd leave the pajamas there. Possibly the suit wasn't the best thing to wear back to Tereza's, but he would have to go to the office for a while tomorrow. He couldn't think how to explain carrying extra clothes across town. Dressed in a suit, he could say his car broke down and he had to walk home, which he hoped would explain why he was out so late.

He just started down the street behind his apartment when he heard a car turning the corner behind him. He stepped into an entryway and held his breath. The black Mercedes rumbled by. The two men in the front seat looked straight ahead. He waited till they disappeared from sight and continued on down the street. Finally he arrived at Tereza's, relieved to reach the shadowy entryway.

She was sleeping again, and he took off his suit and shirt and laid them out carefully on the table. There was only one blanket, and it was covering her. He curled up on the couch and for the first time in a while, began thinking about Erik. Had he made it home without incident? If he were stopped and questioned, would they take him in for more intensive questioning? Would he give up all he knew? The answer to the last would be yes. Anton never intended to let anyone in his group know where he lived, but Erik had been in town one day and saw him going into Mrs. Svobodova's bakery and figured out the rest for himself.

He couldn't worry about any of this now. He needed sleep desperately, and he finally fell into a deep slumber that lasted till the sun was streaming through the high, street-level windows and Tereza was making her way across the room from the bathroom. "Good morning," she said.

"Good morning."

"You don't need to stay here with me. I'll be okay on my own, as long as you bring me some food when you can."

"I'll bring you what I can. You need some decent food to help you heal. I wanted to stay last night to make sure you were going to be okay on the crutches. You realize you can't leave the apartment till your cast is removed and you're walking normally."

She lay down on the bed and hoisted her leg up. "I know. Can you bring me some books? I didn't anticipate having to sit around an apartment for weeks."

"Yes, I'll bring some. Mine are all in Czech. I guess that's okay, though. You handle the language very well."

"That's fine. Just whatever you have. I need to practice reading in Czech. I got up last night and emptied the clothes in the knapsack into the drawers. The camera and all the documents are in there, too, but the camera and extra rolls of film need to be hidden for now. I couldn't think of a good hiding place that I could get to with this cast on my leg."

"I doubt there's a place to keep those things in the apartment."

"Probably not. If we had tape, we could tape it to the underside of some furniture."

"That's probably the first place they'd look. I suppose if they're in here searching your apartment, it's rather immaterial where those things are hidden." He hated sounding pessimistic, but it was better to be realistic about their situation.

"Do you have a place in your apartment where we could keep it till I'm well?"

He'd taken the gun back to the Rosalie and placed it in the secure spot he'd made for it under the dash. He could keep the camera and film under there, too. "I'll take it with me. Not right now, but when I come back later. I have to go to my office today. I'm afraid I'm attracting too much attention by

39

staying away from there. I'll be back sometime later. I wonder if someone put food in the cabinet."

"Who would have come in here and put food in the cabinet?"

"Members of the resistance have ways of doing things that need to be done. A locked door is no deterrent. When it was learned that you'd been injured and would be stuck here in the apartment for a period of time, someone might have decided to take action while you were still at the doctor's office."

He found a can of green beans, a can of beets, and a box of crackers. He ate a couple of the crackers and put the box beside her on the bed. "Can I get you a glass of water?"

"I had some in the bathroom. I need to get up and move around occasionally, or I'll get too weak to ride a bicycle up to the palace."

He went to the bathroom and changed from his pajamas to the shirt and suit. "I have to go now. I'll be back as soon as I can. I'll lock the door, and remember, don't answer if anyone knocks. Do you want me to open some of these windows to let a little fresh air in?"

"I'll do it later. I think it's still a little chilly outside. After all, I'm from Texas."

"Don't say it. Don't even think it. You're from the Sudetenland in Western Czechoslovakia."

With that warning he walked directly to his office on Tynska Street. One of the partners, Anton's best friend, stood in the reception area talking to the receptionist. "Josef. How's it going?"

"Quiet. Too quiet. Not much business lately. I put a note on your desk from one of your clients. Old Mr. Kopecky. He wanted you to call him."

"He always wants me to call him. If the calls would generate any real business, I wouldn't mind. He just wants to complain about his son, whom he calls a wastrel. He seems to think I can do something about the kid's spending."

"I want to show you something in my office."

They went to Josef's cubbyhole of an office, where Josef gestured for him to sit down in the client chair. "I thought I ought to let you know the others are complaining about your staying away from the office so much."

"What difference can it possibly make to them? We're not partners in the real sense of the word. I pay my share of the rent and other expenses here, which is all they need to be concerned about. They keep the income from their work, and I keep the income from mine."

"They think that if you were here more, it would create the look of a busier office, which in turn would generate more business."

"I'll talk to them. If they know of someone else they'd prefer to have here, I'll go out on my own."

"If you go, I'm going with you. They know you have income from a trust fund and that you don't really need to work. They think you're spending all your time with Eliska Muller, and I've encouraged them to think that."

Anton understood his meaning—it left little doubt that Josef was sure he was involved with the resistance. For all Anton knew, Josef might be involved also. He'd talk to the other two when he got a chance. They were out of the office several days this week to work out a trust for a well-to-do client they had managed to find.

Anton went into his own cubbyhole and was lifting the phone to call Mr. Kopecky when Eliska walked in. She didn't look pleased. "Where have you been? I've gone by your apartment three times in the last two days and you're never there. I want you to go to a party with me Saturday."

"Where is it?"

"At a friend's house. It starts at nine."

"You'll have to give me the address and I'll meet you there."

She waved her hand in a dismissive gesture. "Don't worry about it. Just come to my place. We can get a ride with people who can take us home with no problem. You can stay with me that night."

"Who are these people who can get us home with no problem?"

"There'll be a couple of German officers there. Their driver can take us."

The revulsion he felt at socializing with German officers showed on his face.

"They're decent people. We might as well make the most of this occupation. After all, it doesn't hurt to know people who can do things for you."

She was sleeping with one or both of them, he supposed. "Let me think about it. Can you come by this evening and spend the night? I'll let you know then."

"Of course. Someone will drop me off, and it might be late. I'll bring some food if I can."

She came around the desk and kissed him. "Till tonight."

The thought of socializing with Nazis was repulsive, and more than that, he felt somehow as if he would be vulnerable, as if he might somehow reveal his affiliation with the resistance. On the other hand, such a contact might be useful, or Eliska might be unwittingly useful. She was a gossip, and she loved to impress him with tidbits about her circle of friends. He mostly ignored these in the past, but it was now time to start paying attention.

He called old Mr. Kopecky and sympathized with him about his free-spending son. And this time, the old man finally wore down his resistance—he agreed to talk to the young man. He was sure such a talk would have no effect whatsoever on young Kopecky, but maybe he'd be a possible recruit for the resistance. It might give him a purpose in life other than spending his father's money.

He left a few minutes before three to walk to the Café Slavia for the rendezvous with his contact. At the café, they acted like acquaintances having a coffee together. They always avoided the large windows at the front that looked out on the river and chose a table close to the back. His contact was already there when Anton arrived, and he sat down opposite him.

The man was reading a newspaper, and he laid it on the table. "Nice weather we're having."

"It's great, but some clouds are building out there. We may have some rain tonight."

"The paper says so. We haven't had as much as usual this month, and we need some."

There was never much to talk about, since they didn't know each other and were only pretending, and Anton knew it was useless at this point to press for more information about the plan for the Skoda Munitions Works. When the time came, they would let him know. So instead, he said, "Is your family well?"

The waitress interrupted with their coffee, which was a weak excuse for the robust coffee they were used to in the pre-war days, but that's what they got everywhere now if they were able to get coffee at all.

The contact sipped his. They'd drink it black, as no cream or sugar was available. "My family is very well, thanks. And yours?"

"The same. Trying to make the best of things."

They chatted in this vein for a while, and then the contact said, "I must get back to the office. Would you like the paper? I've finished with it."

"Yes, thanks. I haven't seen one today."

Anton sat for a while, finishing his coffee and looking at the front page. There was a glowing account of the Luftwaffe bombings of London and the success of the German Navy in the North Atlantic. It was impossible to tell how much was true, but it was sickening, regardless.

He finished his coffee and returned to the office, where he put the newspaper in the top drawer of his desk. The other two partners had come in, and he went directly to their offices and asked them to come to his. "Josef tells me you're not happy with the fact that I haven't been in the office much lately."

They both looked uncomfortable with being confronted directly about the situation, and assured him that his absence wasn't a big problem, that they had simply mentioned it.

"If you feel there's someone else you'd rather have share the office with you, I'll be glad to strike out on my own. It might be for the best."

Karel Brazda cleared his throat. "I'd rather you'd stay. You pay your share, and that's the most important thing."

Vaclav Kovar nodded. "I agree. Sorry—we didn't mean to upset you. It was just talk."

"Good. We all agree, then, that the present arrangement is working for now. If you have any other concerns, let's talk them over." The two shook Anton's hand and went back to their offices. He cleared up the rest of the work on his desk and went home for the day with his newspaper tucked under his shirt.

When he arrived, he found the coded message in small figures beneath an ad for women's dresses. He took out the book of Kafka short stories and decoded the message. "Postponement okay. Please advise when transaction will begin." He was relieved that the mission was still on. His worry had been that they would decide to extract Tereza and scrap the whole thing. He didn't think she would be thrilled about that, either. His main worry now was obtaining enough food to keep them both alive.

He tore the sheet from the paper where the coded numbers had been written and burned it in the sink along with his translation. He folded the rest of the paper and put it on the bookshelf. He heard a car door close in the street in front of the bakery and looked out to see a dark car driving away in the gathering twilight. He heard someone on the stairs, and Eliska turned her key in the lock and came in.

"What's burning?"

"I thought you said you were going to be late." Thank God she hadn't barged in while he was doing the translation or burning the documents.

"I changed my mind. Are you cooking?"

"No, I started to heat some water for tea, and I laid the newspaper too close. It caught fire."

She was looking at him, and he couldn't decide whether it was with suspicion or whether she thought he was disgustingly stupid. He hoped it was the latter. "Well, can we have some tea? I haven't had any in ages."

"I discovered after I put the water on that I'm out. Sorry. It's been a long day."

"What happened today?"

"Just the usual hassles at the office. Old Mr. Kopecky giving me the same problems."

She set her purse on the counter and took out a can of smoked oysters and a box of crackers. "So you actually made an appearance at the office?"

She must be shopping the black market. Where else would she find smoked oysters? Most likely her maid was doing the shopping. Or maybe the items came from a German friend. He wished he could save some for Tereza, but he doubted that would be possible. "I spent most of the day at the office. I had one meeting with a client outside the office."

"Are you hungry?"

"Very much so."

"You know what they say about oysters. They're good for the libido."

"My libido is just fine, with or without oysters." He scooped her up and carried her to the bed.

CHAPTER SIX

Tereza woke up and looked at the clock that had been in the apartment when she arrived. It was almost noon. But what day was it? Was it just this morning that Anton had given her the box of crackers and left dressed in a suit? He was on his way to his office, he said. The crackers were still beside her in the bed. She got up and made her way on the crutches to the bathroom and her toothbrush, which had come along with her in the jump suit. It was beginning to get stuffy in the apartment, and she opened windows on the three sides of the room that had windows.

She would eat some crackers and some of the green beans for lunch, provided she could find a can opener. She went to the drawers under the cabinet and found some assorted tableware of varying patterns. There was also a serrated knife, a serving spoon, and a can opener. She realized how hungry she was once she got the can open, and she devoured half of the beans with several crackers.

It was important to keep the leg up to keep the swelling down, and she went back to bed after she washed the bowl and fork she used. She wasn't sleepy now, and she wished she had some of Anton's books. Probably a better use of the afternoon would be to try to remember everything that had happened to her since she signed up as an Army nurse in December of forty-one, since a lot would depend on her mental abilities once she recovered and started work at the palace.

She had been involved in basic training when a man came to see her. They called her into the base commander's office at Fort Sam Houston. The man explained that his name was Mr. Smith, and that he represented an agency of the government she'd never heard of and now couldn't remember the name of. The word "coordinator" was part of the agency's name, she was sure of that much. She had been singled out because she spoke both Czech and German. He questioned her extensively about her ability to speak, understand and read the languages, and she explained that her reading ability in Czech wasn't good, but was better in German. The German alphabet was similar to English with a few exceptions, and she had studied German in college.

She spent almost four hours with him. He explained that they were offering her a covert position which would be dangerous, more so than her duties would be as a nurse, but that she could be more valuable to the Allies' cause in Czechoslovakia. Everything would be furnished—documents, money, and ration cards. Her cover would consist of the fabrication that she came from the Bohemian area called the Sudetenland, which was inhabited by many people of German descent. One parent was German, the other Czech, therefore the ability to speak both languages.

Her parents had died in a fire and left her a small trust fund, administered by a law firm in Prague. They would pay her rent and give her cash for other expenses. Food would be scarce, but she might have access to some at the Cernin Palace, near the Prague Castle Complex, headquarters of the Reich Protector and SS. She would work on the cleaning staff there.

She agreed to the assignment, and when basic training was complete, she was called in to the base commander's office and told that she would be working at the post hospital until further notice. She had expected Mr. Smith to show up and whisk her away for more training, but she went to work at the hospital as directed and wondered what was happening to the assignment Mr. Smith had described. Perhaps the delay had something to do with the assassination of Reinhard Heydrich and the terrible reprisals that took place in Czechoslovakia afterward. They had heard the news at Fort Sam.

It was several months later when Mr. Smith came to take her away to a place called Catoctin Mountain Park. He had explained that she would now be with the Office of Strategic Services, which had replaced the first agency he told her he represented.

She reached for her crutches and got up for a drink of water while she thought about this agency change. She still couldn't remember the name of the first agency he described, but if this was the only thing she'd forgotten, she'd be pleased. She was never told why it took so long to get her transferred to the OSS, but she had assumed, when she heard of the agency change, that it was because of reorganization.

Her training at Catoctin was somewhat of a blur, but maybe that was because it flew by so fast and she wasn't permitted to take notes. The main thing she remembered, and remembered clearly, was the use of the camera and changing the film. The rest would come when needed, she was sure.

She got up again and took another pain pill. Before it caused her to become drowsy, she'd try to remember what came after the training at Catoctin. She remembered getting on a plane somewhere. She had a parachute; that much she knew. And thinking about the parachute, she remembered training in parachute jumping at Catoctin. Beyond the plane ride, she couldn't remember anything until she woke up in the trunk of the Rolls Royce, staring at one of the most attractive faces she'd ever seen.

This was just as good a time as any to think about the man who was now her lifeline to food. He was attractive—handsome, yes, but more than that. He was rugged and virile. It would be a mistake to become involved with him. She was twenty-four, and he looked as if he were in his mid-thirties. He was too old for her. For all she knew, he had a girlfriend or a wife. But more importantly, her entire concentration would have to be focused on the mission. Distractions could prove deadly.

She had no idea how long she'd be here—had they told her somewhere along the way, and she'd forgotten that, too? It might be for the duration of the war. She'd be in Prague till someone told her she was leaving. She'd concentrate on learning to read in Czech, beginning with learning the alphabet. The small dictionary she brought in the jump suit would help. It seemed as if it were more important to read in German, but that was no problem. She had taken two years of German while in nurse's training. She would read Anton's books in Czech and keep her mind active.

The pill was beginning to take effect now, and the pain in her leg was easing. As drowsiness overcame her, she said to herself, "I'm Tereza Valentova from the Sudetenland. My parents died in a fire, and I came to Prague looking for work. I worked as a translator for a while, but that job ended when the Germans arrived. After that, all I could find was a cleaning job at the palace. I will not become involved with Anton Janak."

#

A knock at the door woke her. Anton hadn't said anything about anyone coming by, and he said he would keep a key and let himself in. She wouldn't be able to see anything from her windows—they were at street level and her door was at basement level. She heard the knock again. She pulled the blanket over her head and pulled a pillow on top of her in the hope that she would look like an unmade bed if the caller went back up the stairs and looked in the window. Then she heard someone ascending the stairs and going down the street. It couldn't have been the Nazis. They would have broken the door down.

The next time she woke, Anton was standing beside the bed, looking down at her. "Have you eaten something? How are you feeling?"

"I'm okay. Someone knocked on the door today. We had discussed the fact that I shouldn't answer, so I kept still until they went away. Do you have any idea who it was?"

"There's a young man who'll be installing a phone for you. He was due to come next week. He's one of us, so you can let him in, but I need to let you know exactly when he's coming. I'll check and see if that's who came today. Have you had something to eat?"

"I ate some crackers and some of the green beans for lunch. You must eat the rest—they're on the counter. I saved them for you."

"You mustn't save things for me. I want you to eat as much as you can. I brought you a few smoked oysters—three, to be exact, and a few crackers. That's all I managed to salvage from a can a friend brought to my apartment. Here, eat these. You need the protein."

"How did your friend get something like this?" She popped one into her mouth.

"I'm not sure, and I was afraid to ask."

She wondered whether it was a girlfriend who brought the oysters. She absolutely would not ask about a girlfriend or whether he was married. All that was totally beside the point and not something she should be giving a second thought to. "However he got them, I'm grateful. They explained the black market to me in training and said we might be able to get food that way. They also said that I might be able to get food at the palace. Maybe I can bring some for you, too."

"Please don't worry about me. You need to eat as much as you can to keep your strength up and heal your wounds. Speaking of wounds, I need to check the cuts the doctor sewed up. He gave me some medicine and bandages for changing and told me to check every day to make sure there's no infection. I'm afraid it's past time to do that."

She unbuttoned the shirtwaist dress to reveal the bandage on her stomach. Fortunately, she had found some ill-fitting underwear in the knapsack and had put it on. Anton removed the bandage and applied some of the medicine Dr. Havelka had given him.

"This wound looks as if it were healing properly. Fortunately, you're a healthy young woman, and you'll heal quickly." He applied a bandage. "Now, your leg."

She pulled the dress up to reveal her right thigh, and he repeated the procedure. "You have quite a bruise on that leg, too. I'll put all this in the chest, and if for some reason I can't get here, you'll need to change the bandages every day. It's just easier if I can do it."

"Have you heard any news of the war?"

"I saw a paper earlier, but unfortunately, all we get is Nazi propaganda. We can't be sure any of it's true. I'd love to have a radio, but they're outlawed. Actually, I have one hidden away, but I'm afraid to use it. My landlady lives in the back of her shop, and I live upstairs. I'm afraid she'd hear it, and that would put her in a bad position."

"What about my rent here? I know they explained about my financial situation, but I can't remember how my rent is to be paid."

"My law firm administers a trust your parents left you. That's the cover story, and that's the sort of thing we need to concentrate on. I paid your rent three months in advance. I'll have cash for you later on, too, when you need it. In the meantime, I'll use it to get food when I can, and maybe I can get some clothes, or have the doctor's wife get them."

"I have enough clothes for now. None of them fit, and I'll have to have some things before I go to work at the palace, but for now I'm okay. I won't be going anywhere and you're the only one who'll see me except for the telephone man, so I can get by with what I have. Where is this palace, by the way?"

"It isn't very far from here. You could walk, but you'll have a bicycle. You may have to walk it up the hill if it's too steep for you, but at least you can coast down."

"Has the doctor given any indication of how long it'll take till I can get started at my assignment?"

"He said six to eight weeks, but if your leg heals as fast as the tears he sewed up, my guess would be six. Are you eager to get started?

"I'm eager, and I'm nervous. I hope I can remember everything I need to know."

CHAPTER SEVEN

Zita came home in a panic. "The Gestapo is searching the area. I saw them in the next block. We have to do something with Gustav, and fast."

Adelka took the shopping bag from her. "Go upstairs. Get him into one of the old housedresses I left in the closet up there, and my garden shoes. Tie his head up in a kerchief. Then get him down here as quickly as possible so he can be cutting up the potatoes for soup when they arrive. He's my cook, and his name will be Ivana Orlova. Go, quickly!"

Zita and Gustav were just coming down the stairs when Adelka heard a knock at the door. She looked at the young man and decided it might work. It would have been better to hide him somewhere, but she hadn't been able to think of a secure place on such short notice. She took a deep breath. "Answer the door, Zita. I'll get Ivana started in the kitchen."

Gustav followed her, and she dumped the three potatoes from the shopping bag into the sink. "Wash those, and then cut them up on this board. We leave the skins on; no need to waste anything. Put them in this pan when you're through. Take your time, though. The job needs to last till the Gestapo leaves." She heard Zita and the officers coming down the hall.

"These gentlemen are here to search the house, Miss."

Two men stood beside Zita. One was a member of the Gestapo, the other a Prague policeman who obviously was there as translator. She gave them the coldest stare she could muster. "What's the purpose of this?"

"We're looking for a fugitive. He was seen to cross the Charles Bridge recently, so we suspect he's in this area. We need to search your house."

"What makes you think he might be here?"

The policeman was doing the talking. The Gestapo officer hadn't said anything. "We're searching all the houses in Mala Strana. He could have slipped in. Might have climbed up on your roof and entered through an upstairs window."

"What's he wanted for?"

"Crimes against the Protectorate."

Adelka put the shopping bag on the table and came to stand directly in front of the policeman while Gustav continued to struggle with the potatoes at the sink. "What sort of crimes?"

"He's a member of the resistance, and he's dangerous."

"I can assure you, there's no one here but my maid, my cook, and me. Oh, well, help yourself. Zita, show them around. I'll help Ivana with lunch and the groceries." She hoped to God Zita had done something with Gustav's clothes, which she hadn't thought to mention.

They started up the stairs, and she could hear the policeman speaking German to the Gestapo officer. Then she heard them going through the upstairs rooms with Zita chattering at them as they went. After several minutes they came back downstairs and searched the rooms on the first floor.

"All clear, Miss Janakova," the officer said as Zita let them out the front door.

So they knew her name. Suddenly, she was trembling. Adelka sat down at the kitchen table and put her head in her hands.

CHAPTER EIGHT

He hadn't worn the tuxedo since he'd gone to a friend's wedding in Pilzen before the war. He had no doubt he could still get into it, what with food rationing. It might be too big. He didn't have a full-length mirror, but it felt as if it fitted him when he put it on. His dress shoes were old, but when he polished them with some ancient paste polish he had in his medicine cabinet, they were acceptable.

He walked to Eliska's house, feeling conspicuous in the tuxedo. She was planning for him to spend the night after the party, and this would simplify matters, since they would be riding with the enemy. He didn't want them to know where he lived. Her house was in the same area as Teta Adelka and the doctor, but on a different street. He'd never been inside, but walked by once to see where she lived. The place was even grander than Teta Adelka's and the doctor's, at least on the outside.

He knocked on her door, and a young woman in a maid's uniform answered. "I'm here to see Mrs. Muller."

"If you'll wait in the library, I'll let her know you're here." She disappeared and was gone for quite a while. When she came back, she said, "Mrs. Muller is upstairs. She wants you to join her there." She walked with him to the staircase. "It's upstairs, down the hallway on the right, first door on the right."

Eliska was seated at a dressing table in a sheer dressing gown, with nothing on underneath. "Maria didn't show you the way up here? It's impossible to get decent help with this damned war on. The butler quit a month ago, and I won't be able to replace him, I'm sure."

"No problem. I found my way. I could smell your perfume down the hallway."

"Not too strong, I hope."

"Just right."

"You're absolutely luscious in that tuxedo. Shut the door and take it off."

He leaned over and kissed her, then untied the ribbon that was holding her gown closed. She began taking off his tuxedo, and he realized the door was still open. He closed it and came back. She tossed his clothes onto a nearby chair as she removed each item and then dropped her gown to the floor. They slipped between the gold satin sheets on her bed, and the caress of the sheets combined with those of Eliska drove all thoughts of war and Nazis out of his mind.

She offered him a cigarette afterward, and he took it gladly. He had run out two days ago and hadn't been able to buy more. He was enveloped in such euphoria with a cigarette, satin sheets, and the satin skin of Eliska touching his that he almost forgot who he was. But not entirely. All this was lovely, but if it wasn't going to bring information he could use, he'd have to think of a way to avoid partying with Nazis.

"Your house is wonderful. All those books in the library—have you read them all?"

"Of course not, silly. This was my parents' house, and that was my father's library. I haven't read any of them. They deeded this house to me when they went to live in the Sudetenland just before the invasion. They have a large estate there."

Early in their affair, when he had walked by her house, he wondered whether she might ask him to come and live with her. It would have been impossible for various reasons, but he had thought she might ask. Later on, he began to guess that he wasn't her only lover, and having him in her house would put a crimp in her style. His vanity caused him to hope he was her favorite.

#

They were picked up an hour later in a black Mercedes driven by a German private who opened the car doors for them and was careful to see that Eliska's long, silky dress of some champagne-colored fabric was safely inside the car before shutting the door. It didn't take long to reach a house that was

56

even more elegant than Eliska's, with a manicured lawn all around.

A U-shaped driveway led to the front entrance, and that's where the young man assisted them from the backseat. Anton rang the doorbell and a butler answered. They were shown into a drawing room that was pure elegance, from the velvet curtains to the Rembrandt over the fireplace. Anton spotted two German officers, both colonels, and the rest of the group wore civilian clothes. He assumed they were Czech.

Eliska introduced him to everyone, and he tried to remember all their names, setting them in his memory with a brief description. The information might be useful later. The colonels were Hans Schiller and Frederich Hesse. Anton suspected, if one of them were Eliska's lover, it would be Schiller. He was handsome in a purely Aryan way, a little over Anton's six feet in height, and gave the impression of being in charge of the room without lifting a finger. Hesse was more jovial, and shook Anton's hand a little longer than was necessary. If you're one of us, it's a pleasure to meet you.

It was a nerve-wracking experience, trying to appear pleasant and at ease in a group where Germans were present. Anton made sure his handshakes were firm and confident, and he hoped his smile appeared to be friendly.

The hostess was a short, stout woman with yellow hair and a beaming smile. Nothing would go wrong at one of her dinner parties. The butler announced that dinner would be served shortly, and she led them into the dining room. Anton found his place at the right hand of the hostess. The stranger would be given the place of honor, and if he proved to be an equal, would be taken into the fold of the anti-Communists, the anti-most-everyone that wasn't rich and of the upper crust.

Eliska was seated near the other end of the table beside Schiller on one side and a woman whose name Anton was trying to remember on the other. A thin woman with her hair piled high, her name was . . . Hasprova. His hostess was Veronika Horakova, and while making small talk with her, he'd try to review the others in the room to establish them in his mind more firmly.

His contacts in the resistance knew about Eliska and the fact that she was married to a German. They knew more than he did about her, probably, and he always assumed they hoped he could acquire helpful information through her. He'd have to make it clear to them that she now wanted to include him in socializing that included German officers. Even more deadly than the Gestapo or the SS was a resistance group suspicious of being sold out.

Mrs. Horakova, at least he assumed she was a Mrs.—even though there was no Mr. Horak around—was saying something to him while his mind was wandering. He pretended he hadn't heard due to the babble going on around them and asked her to repeat.

"What sort of work do you do, Mr. Janak?

"I'm an attorney. I'm in a partnership with three others."

Mrs. Horakova, still beaming, said, "Oh, that's a wonderful profession. Where's your office?"

"It's in Old Town, on Tynska Street."

Old Town. Respectable enough. "Do you have family in Prague?"

"Only an aunt. My parents are deceased, and I'm an only child."

"I know a lady named Adelka Janakova. We go to church together at the cathedral. St. Vitus. Would she be your aunt?"

He didn't want these people to know so much about him, but he couldn't lie. "Yes, that's my Teta Adelka."

"She's a lovely lady. We've been doing volunteer work together for years. She invited the members of our women's circle to her home for tea one afternoon last year. It was charming, and we all enjoyed her beautiful old home. I haven't seen as much of her lately, though, and I hope she isn't ill."

That's because I have her car. "No, she's fine. I'll be taking her to church tomorrow—the late mass. Maybe you'll see her there."

"Yes, I planned to attend late tomorrow also. After a party, you know, it's difficult to make it to the early mass." Soup was being served now, and she didn't say anything more, watching to make sure everything was done correctly. When

58

everyone had been served, "And your father—what did he do?"

"He taught law at Charles University." She would find this more acceptable than the Humanities.

"Is that where you attended?"

"Yes, my partners and I all went there and became friends." *And now the SS is using our law school as a barracks*, he thought. Just one more reason to do everything he could to get them out of Czechoslovakia. The soup was good, a puree of vegetables with plenty of seasoning. He only wished he could take some to Tereza. It would be good for her.

After the soup course, a lamb chop was served with potatoes, Brussels sprouts, and a tasty yeast roll. He hadn't eaten this well since the occupation began. Wine was flowing freely as well, and his glass was refilled frequently. Time to stop with the wine—he wanted to keep his wits about him. Dessert was a chocolate mousse and real coffee, a rich brew that was so good he accepted a second cup.

When everyone was finished, they moved back to the drawing room where a trio had set up in a corner. They began playing a polka, and he saw Eliska skip away in the arms of the other German . . . Hesse, Frederich Hesse. He was having trouble remembering even the names of the Germans. More guests began arriving now, and he saw that he had been among the privileged few invited to dinner before the party.

He should ask someone to dance instead of standing around looking helpless, so he went up to a middle-aged woman who had been at the dinner and she accepted readily. As they whirled around the room, he said, "I'm terribly sorry, but I've forgotten your name. I'm not very good at names, and there were so many thrown at me all at once."

She giggled. "I'm Clara Plankova. I must admit I've forgotten yours too."

"Anton Janak. I'm a friend of Eliska Muller."

"I've known Eliska for years. Her parents are friends of mine."

"Yes, I understand they've moved to the Sudetenland."

Mrs. Plankova put her hand on his arm. "I've heard a rumor that Eliska's divorcing Kurt. Do you suppose there's anything to that?"

Of course he had. His partner was handling it. "I haven't heard anything."

"Then I heard an even newer rumor." She looked around to see if anyone was listening. "Someone told me his family is very upset about the divorce, and they've offered her a place on the Rhine and a lot of money to come to Germany and stay married to Kurt. Catholic, of course, and totally opposed to divorce."

"Really? That's interesting. No, I haven't heard anything about any of this."

Mrs. Plankova was looking at him as if she wondered just how good a friend he was to Eliska if he knew nothing of these rumors. Then the music ended before he had a chance to think of anything else to say, and he escorted the lady back to her seat.

The trio started a waltz, and Eliska came up to him. "This one's mine." She moved smoothly in his arms as he wondered whether he should ask her about the latest rumor or whether he should let her tell him when she was ready. If he decided to bring up the subject, it would be later, back at her house.

"You were dancing with Clara Plankova, the biggest gossip not just in Prague but in all of Czechoslovakia. Did she tell you anything interesting?"

"Not really. Have you heard anything interesting tonight? If I'm going to socialize with these people, I want to know all the dirt."

She laughed. "Stop being sarcastic. Gossip is the last thing you're interested in. I heard something that isn't really gossip, and it made me rather sad. Frederich is being transferred to Norway. He'll be leaving in two weeks."

"Why would anyone want to go to Norway? It's even colder up there than it is here, and winter will be coming on."

"He doesn't want to go—they're sending him."

"I guess that's what life is in the military. You go where they send you."

"Were you ever in service?

"Well before the war. I guess they thought I was too old by the time Germany invaded. I haven't heard from anyone."

"Thirty-three isn't so old. I'm surprised you weren't called back when the invasion began." She whispered the words. "We try not to discuss the invasion in a mixed group such as this."

"How much longer do you think the party will go on?"

"Probably till midnight. Why?"

"Just wondering. I promised my aunt I'd take her to church in the morning, and I want to make sure we'd have time to frolic on those satin sheets between now and then."

Eliska laughed. "There's always time for frolicking. Do you take your aunt to church often? There are still plenty of things I don't know about you."

"I usually take her, because she doesn't like to drive anymore."

"You in church. I can't imagine it."

"I can't imagine it, either, and I usually don't stay. I go back and pick her up later."

The music ended, and they waited on the floor for the next number. "I didn't know you had a car," Eliska said.

"I don't. It's her car." He was revealing more than he wanted to, but he didn't know how to evade the question.

"So you walk to her house and drive from there. Where does she live?"

"Not far from here. A few streets over, a couple of streets down."

"Really? You never told me about her. Right here in my own neighborhood."

"My mind's always on other things when I'm with you."

She squeezed him, and he could feel her breasts pressing against his jacket. "That's sexy," she whispered in his ear.

"Keep that up, and we're going to leave right away."

"It's after ten. I think we can slip out about eleven without anyone noticing."

"The place is getting crowded. No one will miss us."

The trio began playing again, something Anton didn't recognize and didn't want to dance to. "Let's see if we can find something to drink. It's getting warm in here."

"There's champagne punch on the sideboard over there. Let's get some."

They had just arrived at the punchbowl when Col. Schiller walked up and asked Eliska to dance. A maid was serving the punch, and she poured a cup for Anton. A nearby French door opened onto what appeared to be a terrace, and he carried his cup outside. Two people stood at the far end of the terrace. As his eyes adjusted to the dark, he could see it was Col. Hesse and Mrs. Plankova.

They were speaking German and hadn't noticed him. He wished his German were better, and that he could understand more of what they were saying. One thing he did understand. Mrs. Plankova was completing a long sentence, and at the end of it, she said, "Herr Janak."

Anton coughed, and they looked at him. Mrs. Plankova giggled and walked toward him; Hesse followed. "Mr. Janak, I was just telling Col. Hesse what a delightful dancer you are. I see you're taking a break with some of the delicious champagne punch."

"Thank you, Mrs. Plankova. The punch is very good." He found it hard to believe she was describing him as a delightful dancer. Eliska always indicated he was barely adequate on the dance floor. He felt a sudden urge to leave the party as soon as possible. As soon as he got a chance tomorrow, he'd code a message about Hesse being transferred to Norway. The information might not be important—there was no way of telling—but he'd send it regardless.

He went back inside and saw Eliska still clinging to Col. Schiller on the dance floor. Cutting in might be rude, and he didn't want to make an enemy of a German officer. Maybe he could catch her eye. He stood along the sidelines and finished his punch, then went to the sideboard for more. Finally, the music ended, and Eliska appeared at his side. "Can't we get out of here now? I'm hot in this tuxedo, and I'm tired of being sociable."

"I'll get some punch and meet you on the terrace. We can walk around to the front of the building and get the driver to take us home. You'll stay at my place tonight, won't you?"

"I wouldn't miss it. Those satin sheets are almost as exotic as you are." In addition, he didn't want the driver to know where he lived. Not that they would have a problem finding out if they wanted to know. They could follow him home from the office, or simply ask Eliska.

She joined him on the terrace after a while with her little clutch purse under her arm. They sipped punch for a few minutes, then set half-empty cups on the railing and walked around to the front of the house.

"I'm feeling guilty that we're skipping out without telling the hostess thanks and goodnight," he said.

"Don't worry about it. With such a crowd, she'll never notice."

The driver was sitting in the car, and he helped them into the backseat.

All was quiet at Eliska's house; the maid must have gone to bed. They went upstairs to the bedroom, where clothes came off in a pile on the floor. Feeling a little mellow from the champagne punch, they made love slowly and sensuously, and then fell asleep in each other's arms.

CHAPTER NINE

He changed out of his tuxedo and into slacks and a cotton shirt. It would make Teta Adelka happy if he'd attend church with her, but he didn't like to leave the car sitting around with no one in it. His gun and Tereza's camera and film were well hidden under the dash, but if someone really wanted to find something, they could be found. He would make excuses about having to meet someone at the office. She wouldn't approve of his working on Sunday, but he couldn't think of anything else.

He drove to her house and parked out front. He rang the bell, and Zita let him in. "She's waiting for you in the library. I'll fix lunch, so you can eat when you get back from church."

"Thanks, Zita. I'll look forward to that." Zita had her ways of getting food, and Anton wasn't about to question her methods. He could look forward to another decent meal. Teta Adelka always insisted he take leftovers with him, so he'd head directly to Tereza's and feed her. He went to the library and found his aunt sitting with an open book on her lap. She was a reader, and she enjoyed her father's library. Many of the books from Anton's father were on the shelves here too. Anton didn't have room in his apartment for all of them.

He kissed her cheek, and she patted his hand. "Not dressed for church, I see."

"I'll drop you off. I have to go to the office for something. I'll be back to pick you up when it's over."

"You didn't bring your clothes for Zita to wash and iron."

He had explained to her several times that his landlady gladly did his laundry for an extra amount added to the rent. Was she getting forgetful? "My landlady does it, remember? She charges me next to nothing."

65

"You should consider coming here to live with me. You wouldn't have to pay anything. After all, this house and everything in it will be yours when I'm gone. You might as well enjoy it now."

This was something else they had discussed many times. In addition to enjoying his company, she probably wanted him living with her so she could see to his spiritual health. "My place is so convenient for walking to the office. I can't bear to give it up. Besides, I like living in Old Town, getting to know all the streets and restaurants. And don't talk about being gone. I'm counting on having you around for a long time. You're the only relative I have."

"You have the cousins in Cesky Krumlov."

"I haven't seen them in ages. After the war, I'll get back in touch."

#

They drove to the church at the castle complex, and after going through security, he parked as close to the entrance as he could and opened the door for her. "I'll be back when mass is over."

He needed to talk to Jakub, who had been with him the night of the parachute disaster. He and Erik had helped Anton with Tereza then, and now he was supposed to install Tereza's phone. It must have been Jakub who came to her door the other day, although he was supposed to let them know when he was coming and hadn't done that. He worked as a waiter at the Kolkovna.

Anton parked the Rosalie, went inside, and sat at a table in Jakub's section. The restaurant wasn't crowded and probably wouldn't be till after late mass. Jakub came to his table right away. "May I help you, sir?"

"Just coffee. Did you go to Tereza's apartment yesterday?"

"No, I had to work yesterday. I'm off Tuesday and plan to take the phone to her then. I was going to call and let you know."

"Someone knocked on her door, that's all. They knocked twice and went away. I'll let her know you're coming Tuesday. Can we set a definite time?"

"I'll come at noon."

"Better get the coffee now."

If the Nazis had discovered her identity and had come for her, they would have kicked the door down. Possibly it was someone who was knocking at the wrong address. Surely Dr. Havelka wouldn't go by to check on her without letting them know he was coming. Jakub brought the coffee and Anton sipped it slowly. It was weak, nothing like the wonderful brew of last night, but he'd take his time and enjoy it anyway.

When he finished the coffee he drove back to the cathedral and parked. The congregation started leaving soon, and he spotted Teta Adelka chatting with Mrs. Horakova, his hostess of last night. God, he hoped she wouldn't say anything that would cast suspicion on him—about the car, about the fact that he didn't go to his office much these days, or about anything else she might have noticed that he was doing differently, that she didn't understand.

They both came to the car, and he got out, ready to shake hands with Mrs. Horakova. She gave him a hug instead and kissed his cheek. Acceptance into her circle, via Eliska and Teta Adelka. Now he would have to decide whether he really wanted to be a part of her circle.

They chatted briefly in the warm noontime sunshine, and then Mrs. Horakova's butler, doing double duty as chauffeur, drove up and helped her into her car, a much newer Citroen. He ushered Teta Adelka into the Rosalie. "Mrs. Horakova was telling me that you attended a party at her house last night," she said.

How to answer? "I did. She has a wonderful home."

"There's a rumor among the ladies in our group that she socializes with the Germans."

"There were a couple of Germans there. I avoided them." He couldn't think of a better reply.

"How do you know Mrs. Horakova?"

"I didn't know her before the party. A friend asked me to go with her. She was without an escort at the last minute, and I went—just to help her in an awkward situation."

"Is this a girlfriend?"

"No, just a friend." The fact that she hadn't made an issue of his attending a party where Germans were present made him virtually positive she was sure of his involvement with the resistance. She knew him well enough to know he wouldn't attend such a party under normal circumstances.

Zita was waiting to serve lunch when they arrived at the house. They had soup made with a few vegetables and grilled sandwiches made with cheese and a tiny bit of meat of some kind.

Zita poured the leftover soup into a jar and made two sandwiches, which she put into a brown bag. "This is for your supper tonight," she said.

"And what will you and Teta do for supper?"

"I have other things to fix for us. There's a tiny squash, and more cheese. I think there's a potato, too. We have plenty."

Thank goodness for Zita. What would Teta Adelka do without her? "I appreciate all you do here," he said to the maid, "especially the way you go out every day and bring home food." Maybe he should suggest an increase in her salary. If she quit, it would be a disaster. Or maybe he should give her something each week. He took out a handful of korunas and handed them to her. "This is for you."

"Sir, you don't need to do that."

"I want to." And with that, he left.

He drove to his apartment and put the Rosalie away, then went upstairs and created a message about the transfer of Col. Frederich Hesse. When it was coded, he signaled his contact to meet him at three at Our Lady of Victory Church. It would be a pleasant day for a walk across the Charles Bridge into Lesser Town and an excellent diversion for a Sunday afternoon. The contact liked the church, Anton could tell, and always crossed himself with the holy water on the way in.

He put the food in Tereza's knapsack, which he had been keeping with him, along with a selection of books from his bookshelf. Maybe he'd bring some from Teta Adelka's next time, something that would be easier for her to read.

He walked to her apartment and let himself in. She was sitting up in bed, leaning on a pillow and writing in a small notebook. She must have had it with her when she jumped, in one of the pockets of the jumpsuit. "What are you writing?"

"I'm keeping a journal, but nothing that could be used against us. Just a record of the date, what's happening outside my windows, whether I saw you, what I ate. Things like that. I don't mention you by name."

"I suppose it's okay. Just be careful." He took the books from the knapsack and laid them on her bed. "I'll try to come up with a better selection next Sunday."

"These will be fine for practicing reading Czech."

"I have some soup and sandwiches here. Are you hungry?"

"Always. Thank you."

He poured the soup into a pot and put it on the hotplate. He put the sandwiches on a plate. "Do you want to come to the table?"

"Yes, I need to move around." She got up and made her way to the table on the crutches.

He opened the cabinet. "Would you like this soup in a mug? It would be easier that way."

"Yes, please. You must eat one of these sandwiches."

"I just ate. I can't eat anything more. It's all for you. I have a couple of teabags. Would you like some tea?"

She was devouring one of the sandwiches. "I'd love some tea. This can't be easy for you. You were expecting a healthy young woman to arrive and go to work immediately at the palace. Instead, you have to worry about getting food for me when you probably have difficulty getting enough for yourself."

"This work is one long string of difficulties. Things crop up all the time that cause me to wonder how I'm expected to deal with them. I just do the best I can. It's not as if I have a boss standing over my shoulder and directing my every move. So don't worry, you aren't my first problem and you won't be my last. Not all of my problem cases manage to save my life with a pitchfork. For that I'll always be grateful."

She smiled. "Sometimes pure instinct takes over. That's what happened in the barn. I don't even know how I got from the car and around to where that huge man was choking you."

"I'm just glad you managed. And I hope your instincts are always going to be that helpful." He poured boiling water into the cups with the tea bags and took them to the table. He just sat down when they heard a tap at the door. "Does that sound like the same knock you heard the other day?"

"Exactly. I'm glad you're here."

"Well, I'm going to see who it is." He went to the door and opened it. Erik was standing there, ready to knock again. He looked surprised to see Anton.

Anton grabbed him by the shirt and dragged him inside. "What the hell are you doing here?"

"I just wanted to see how Tereza is doing. I wanted to come and see her."

"How did you know where she lives?"

"I followed you the other day."

Anton was having difficulty resisting the urge to beat the stupidity out of this teenager. "Don't you realize you could be jeopardizing this entire operation?"

Erik was sulking now. "You told me to get a girlfriend."

"I didn't mean Tereza, you idiot!"

"Well, you're here. You come here, so why can't I?"

"I have a reason to be here. My parents were friends of Tereza's parents. Her relatives asked me to look after her when she came to Prague to find a job."

"Really?"

"No, not really, you idiot! It's her cover!" Anton was managing to keep his voice down with the most extreme effort. He grabbed Erik's shirt again. "Get out of here. Go back to your parents' farm and stay there. Don't come in town again unless I tell you to. Forget you ever saw this place. Do you understand?"

Erik nodded, and Anton pushed him to the door, shoved him outside, and slammed the door. He sat down again. "Jesus! If I were some people in this movement, he'd be dead before the day's over."

Tereza nodded. She understood perfectly. "I think you made an impression on him. It's obvious he respects you, so I hope he does as you told him."

"If he ever shows up here again, let me know immediately. Jakub is coming Tuesday at noon to install your phone. I'll be here when he comes, and I'll give you my number at home and at the office. You need to memorize both numbers and burn the slip. Do you have matches?"

"Yes, I have plenty. I'll burn the paper in the sink and wash the ashes down."

Anton was calmer now, and he felt the need to explain a little further about Erik and Jakub. "Did you hear of an assassination that occurred here in Prague? I think it made the news everywhere."

"Of course. We heard about it when I was still working at the hospital at Fort Sam."

"I just want you to know both Erik and Jakub have been very useful in our work. I can't say any more. Now if we can just rein in their youthful lack of judgment, maybe they won't get us all detained, tortured, and killed."

He had to finish his tea now so he could be on time to meet the contact. He found himself wishing Tereza could walk across the Charles Bridge with him. He thought about how much she'd enjoy Our Lady of Victory Church and the famous statue of the Infant Jesus. He wondered whether she was Catholic, whether she was a believer. A woman like her, well, she could almost make a believer out of him.

CHAPTER TEN

The weeks had dragged by. The doctor had come to see her twice—once to remove the stitches from her wounds, and once to check her leg. She had heard the doctor's name mentioned at a checkpoint, but she wiped it out of her mind. There was no need to know. He was impressed with the way her leg had healed, and he removed the cast. He said she'd be ready to walk without the crutches by the end of the sixth week. He wanted her to get outside and do some walking on the street, and she was more than ready. She asked Anton for money, and he gave her what seemed to be a fortune.

Reading in Czech had been easier than she imagined. She read everything Anton brought with occasional help from her dictionary. She always carried a book with her now when she went out in the afternoons. She stopped at one café or another, found a cozy corner, and read while drinking weak coffee. One time, at the Café Slavia, she had seen Anton having coffee with another man. They ignored her, and she had pretended not to recognize him.

After two weeks of walking every day, the doctor was coming this evening to see how she was doing. She had managed to buy a small cake, and Anton had given her a few teabags she'd been hoarding, so she was planning a celebration if the doctor said she could ride a bicycle and go to work.

The doctor arrived, pronounced her leg healed, and she insisted he stay for tea and cake. He appeared to be charmed by the idea. She had found an ancient linen tablecloth with a lace border in a second-hand shop, and she spread it over the table before cutting the cake and serving the tea. She had no napkins, but with all the shortages, she hoped this would be acceptable. There would be no war talk. She chatted with him

73

about all the things she'd seen while walking the city for two weeks, and he recommended many more places she should investigate. She didn't mention the ever-present Nazis she always encountered in the streets and cafes. It was a small tea party with a man whose name she didn't know. The only drawback to the celebration was that Anton wasn't there.

#

She pushed her bicycle up the hill to the castle area. Before her injuries, riding it would have been no problem, and she was sure that with weeks of riding, she'd be back in shape. After passing through security, she went to the entrance of the Cernin Palace as Anton had told her to do, wearing the identification tag he had furnished. He had insisted she leave the camera behind for at least a week, maybe longer. "I'm to see Olga Klimanova. I'm a member of the cleaning staff."

One of the guards at the door looked over her documents then took her inside to a room off a long hallway where she was searched by a heavy-handed woman in uniform. Thank God she hadn't brought the camera. She wondered whether she'd be searched every day, and if so, how she'd ever be able to bring it. After the search, the woman directed her farther down the hallway to the last door on the right. She knocked and heard a woman's voice shout, "Come in."

Olga Klimanova was seated at a desk covered by stacks of papers. She was a stout woman with dark hair pulled back from her face. She stood and came forward to shake Tereza's hand. "You're Tereza Valentova. I'm Olga Klimanova, as you already know. Call me Olga. You're here to work with the cleaning crew, and you'll be assigned at first on the lower level of the palace. I'll show you around, and then you can get started."

Tereza suspected that someone on the staff at the palace had arranged for her employment there, and she wondered if it were Olga. Something else she didn't need to know at present, something that would be better for everyone concerned if she didn't know. "Thanks. I'm eager to get started. My rent is coming due, and I need the money. I was lucky to get this job."

They went to the hallway and down a set of stairs to the lower level. The first room they visited was a large supply room lined with shelves stacked with various forms and office supplies. On the far side of the room was what Tereza took to be a mimeograph machine where a young man was working. "You'll dust everything in here," Olga said. "Just be careful not to rearrange anything. Our bosses are particular about how everything is lined up down here."

"What will I use for the dusting?"

"You'll have a cart with all your supplies. It has your name on it. There's a large lamb's wool duster you'll use in here. There's a mop and bucket for the floor when you're through." They approached the man, who had been watching them all the time they were in the room. "This is Wilhelm. He operates the mimeograph and takes supplies upstairs when they're ordered. Try not to get in his way."

"I'll try. Hello, Wilhelm."

He shook her hand. "Pleased to meet you."

Tereza saw that he was young, probably eighteen, and was tall and thin with blonde hair. Remembering her training at Catoctin in German military rank, she saw he was a private. She followed Olga from the room and down the hallway to several small offices that would be her responsibility. At the end of the hallway they came to a large storage area where the carts were kept. Her name was already on hers. A sink stood in a corner of the room—this was where she would fill her mop bucket.

"Could I write down the room numbers where I'm supposed to clean? I don't want to miss anything."

"You're not allowed to have paper, pencil, or pen. You'll have to memorize them. We'll go over them again as we go back to my office."

Olga certainly was allowed to have paper, considering the stacks on her desk. When they returned to the office, Olga asked her to read and sign a sheet which outlined her duties and listed the rooms that were her responsibility. She memorized them quickly. "You'll be here at seven in the morning and work until four. If you finish with your assigned rooms, come back to me and I'll find something for you to do

75

till your shift ends. You'll be searched on leaving, and the woman who does the searching isn't on duty till four. The door will be locked until then, and no one goes out until they're searched."

Tereza went back downstairs to the cart room, got her cart, and filled the mop bucket. She'd start with the supply room and clean the offices next.

Wilhelm was gone when she returned to the supply room, and he came in after she started dusting. "What was your name again? I've forgotten already."

"Call me Tereza. Is it okay if I call you Will?"

"Sure. Some of my friends call me Will. You speak German very well."

"I'm from the Sudetenland."

"I've heard of it. A lot of Germans live there, don't they?"

"Yes, my mother was of German descent. I learned both languages growing up."

He gave the impression of being a little slow in his thinking, which could be a useful trait if she were ever to have a chance to see what he was printing on the mimeograph. A huge metal cabinet stood against the wall at the side of the room. A padlock secured the doors. It would be interesting to see what was in that locked cabinet. She finished the dusting and mopped the floor when Will left to deliver a ream of typing paper to someone upstairs.

Tereza moved on to the offices. There wasn't much to be seen in any of them—no loose papers lying around. Three of the six were occupied by men in uniform talking on phones, but they hung up immediately when she came in and left so she could clean. She had finished her duties by three forty-five, and she wondered if Olga had assigned a light load to give her time to look in desk drawers and check out what was going on with the mimeograph.

She returned her cart and took her time rinsing her mop and bucket. She wanted to go outside to shake out the duster, but she didn't know how to get out except through the main door, and she wouldn't be able to go out there without being searched. She shook the duster over a waste basket and hoped that was good enough. She didn't want to be fired for incompetence before getting started doing any of the real work.

Olga wasn't in her office when Tereza knocked on the door, so she stood in the hallway till the older woman appeared. "I'm through now, but I'm wondering—is there someplace outside where I can shake the dust out of my duster?"

"Come, I'll show you." They went back downstairs, past the cart room, and down a second hallway with a door leading outside. They were in a patio that was enclosed by a high brick wall. "Bring your duster out here. You can whack it against the wall. You can come out here and eat your lunch, also, but you need to make that quick. Did you bring some lunch today?"

"I didn't have anything to bring, but I have a little money left. I'll try to find something this evening."

"You can leave now. It's almost four. Go out the way you came in. Just remember, there will be a search on the way out, also."

Tereza wondered how she'd ever be able to smuggle a camera in or any information out with two daily searches. Maybe it was just for the first week. The woman who searched her on the way in was in her office with the door open, and two women were waiting outside while she searched a third. Tereza stood in line behind the other two. A guard stood to the side, watching the line.

The one next to her turned. "I'm Natalie, and this is Pavlina. You're new, aren't you?"

"Yes. I'm Tereza. I'm assigned to the lower floor."

"You'll move up eventually. Sometimes there's an opportunity for some food if you're on one of the upper floors."

"That would be helpful." She wanted to ask whether the searches would go on forever, but she was afraid the searcher would hear. Both these women gave the impression of having been around a while, so that probably answered her question. When her turn came, the searcher was even more thorough than she had been in the morning. There were many indignities to be suffered in her line of work, obviously, but she would suffer them gladly if she could make a difference.

She had chained her bicycle with a combination lock in a thicket of trees, and she unlocked it, threw the chain into the basket, and coasted down the hill, feeling free as a bird. Anton had delivered the bicycle yesterday—actually he rode it to her apartment—and she kept it just inside her door. She could walk to the palace, but the bicycle made it easier, especially coasting back to Old Town at the end of a day of cleaning.

She took the bicycle inside, stood it by the door with the kickstand, and got her money and coupon cards for shopping. A few small stores were located in the area, and she visited all of them. There was never any butter, and how she longed for real butter. She got two potatoes and a little bread and returned home. She was starving by this time, and she quickly made some potato soup with water, leaving the skins on. Fortunately she had some salt that Anton had given her. She ate some of the bread while the potatoes were cooking and put the rest back for breakfast and lunch tomorrow. The soup was filling, if nothing else.

She was washing dishes when Anton came in. He never knocked, knowing that she wouldn't answer a knock, so she always dressed in the bathroom. "How did it go today?" he asked.

"Very well, except that I was searched on the way in and on the way out. It looks like that will continue, because two women who appeared to have been there for some time were being searched also. There's a mimeograph machine, and I might be able to take photos of what's printed on it, but I don't know how I'll be able to take a camera in, even as small as that one is, or bring anything out."

"Don't worry. It'll be taken care of eventually. It's probably better that you don't look in any desk drawers yet, or try to check out what's going on with the mimeograph machine. Get used to the routine for a couple of weeks."

"The lady named Olga told me that I should report back to her if I finished my work before four, and she'd find something else for me to do. Maybe I'll get an opportunity to expand my horizons. I clean a supply room where there are a lot of forms as well as the mimeograph machine, and then some smaller offices. The offices have desks and phones, but no papers anywhere. There were men in some of the offices today, and they stopped talking on the phones as soon as I came in. All the desks in those rooms appear to have a locked drawer, because there's a keyhole."

She had been rattling on, trying to avoid the thought that in spite of her determination to avoid getting involved with Anton, she found herself wanting him desperately. Maybe it was just that she'd had so much exposure to him in all the weeks he'd been looking after her, but she didn't want to avoid it any longer. If they'd given her any advice or rules about this in her training, she couldn't remember them. She did wish he'd make the first move, but if he didn't, she would. "I still have a couple of tea bags. Would you like some tea?"

"Have you eaten?"

"I had some bread and potato soup. How about you?"

"Not yet. I came directly from the office. My landlady will have something for me when I get back to my apartment. We have an arrangement—I pay her extra for doing my laundry and giving me some food in the evenings. She almost always has something. I give her part of my coupons."

"How about that tea?"

They were sitting at the table now. He reached out and took her hand. "Maybe later." He kissed her fingertips. "You've probably figured out by now that I'm falling for you. I tried to avoid this, but I'm afraid it was inevitable."

She was smiling. "Come to bed with me."

In her bed, among the sturdy cotton sheets, he held her and kissed her. All thoughts of their age difference were gone, and she put her arms around his neck. "I need you," she said, as he drew her to him.

#

Tea never tasted as good as it did this evening. They sat together at the table, and her entire body was still filled with the ecstasy of their lovemaking. He didn't say anything, just held her hand and drank his tea. She knew he'd have to leave soon. She wished he could stay; she wished they could hibernate here in her apartment till the war was over. His staying wouldn't be a good idea, she knew, and the last thing she wanted to do now was anything that would endanger them. She kissed him at the door and told him goodnight.

CHAPTER ELEVEN

The streets had taken on a soft glow as he walked back to his apartment. Was it just the last of the sunlight being reflected down from the clouds, or was it that making love to Tereza permanently altered his vision? He was smiling. Anyone who met him would think him demented, walking along and smiling to himself. Reality would come crashing down on him soon enough, he knew, but for now he was smiling.

When he got to the bottom of his stairs he could see that the lights were on in his apartment. Eliska was there. Eliska or someone who had broken in. Whoever it was, he was certain he didn't want to see them. He couldn't make love to Eliska tonight. He didn't think he could ever make love to her again. He went into his garage and closed the door after him. Eliska didn't know about the garage or the Rosalie. He got into the back seat of the car and curled up. Before long he was dreaming of Tereza.

#

He woke up in the middle of the night feeling stiff and cold. He left the garage and went to the bottom of the stairs. The light in his apartment was off. If Eliska had gone to bed there, she'd be waiting for him in the morning anyway, so he climbed the stairs and let himself in. The apartment was empty. He found no note, and nothing appeared to have been disturbed. He found bread and cheese on his table, and he ate it before going to bed. Maybe it was simply Mrs. Svobodova bringing his food, but then she always came earlier, before it was necessary to turn on a light.

#

He woke up early and went to the office. Josef was already there and came pecking on his door as soon as he was seated behind his desk. "You'd never guess what's happened—or perhaps you already know. Eliska Muller is calling off the divorce. She came in yesterday and told me to forget the whole thing. She's reconciling with her husband. She left this for you." He handed Anton an envelope.

So Clara Plankova's gossip had actually been true. He took out the note and read, in her flamboyant handwriting, "Darling—I wanted so desperately to see you last night. I'm leaving on the train this afternoon for Germany. Kurt's family has made me an offer I can't turn down. Hans Schiller will be looking after my house. Please meet me for lunch at 1 p.m. at the Slavia, and then ride with me to the station. I'll always love you. Eliska."

He looked up at Josef. "Not only is she calling off the divorce, she's leaving town."

"Where's she going?"

"To Germany. Apparently his family is dead-set against the divorce, and has offered her a house and quite a bit of money to get back together with him."

"Won't she have trouble traveling into Germany?"

"When you have as much money as Kurt's family has, arrangements can be made. I assume they've been made. She's leaving by train this afternoon. I'll have lunch with her and see her off at the station."

"I'm sorry, Anton. I don't know exactly what your feelings toward her were, but I know this must be a blow."

"I was fond of her, and I'll miss her." He realized this was true, even though, because of his involvement with Tereza, he was glad Eliska was leaving.

"Old Mr. Kopecky's been calling you again. He wants to know whether you've seen his son."

"I'm planning to go to his son's place this morning. I'll call the old man back after I've seen the son. He's in an apartment not far from here."

Anton wrote a couple of letters in longhand and cleared up the rest of the work on his desk. He took the letters to Martina, their receptionist and secretary, for typing. "I'm leaving now, and I'll be gone till sometime later this afternoon."

Anton wondered whether society's rebels and black sheep made good resistance workers. He'd take a close look at the young man he was going to visit to see whether he was someone to be mentioned to Anton's contact. He walked to the apartment of the young Mr. Kopecky and knocked on the door. The place was in a run-down building in a run-down part of town. Nobody answered. He knocked again, much louder this time. He was about to walk away when he heard noises inside. Someone was coming to the door.

Anton could tell he had waked the man. His hair was tousled, he had several days' growth of beard, and he didn't smell good. An alcoholic, Anton was sure of it. "What do you want?"

"I'm Anton Janak, your father's attorney. May I come in?"

"Suit yourself."

Anton followed him into a cluttered sitting room. An empty wine bottle was turned on its side on the coffee table. He sat on a filthy loveseat. "Your father is concerned about you."

"Why is that?"

"You aren't working, and he's spending money on you. His resources aren't limitless."

"I can't find a job."

"I know they're not easy to find right now, but you'd encounter more opportunities if you'd make sure you're looking your best when you go out job hunting." The man wouldn't be stable enough for any kind of undercover work.

"I went down to the Skoda Plant at Pilsen. It was just my luck that the manager I talked to there was a man I used to work for here in Prague. He threw me out without even giving me a chance to ask for work."

"Where were you working for him here?"

"I worked for an agency that furnished janitors for office buildings."

"Maybe you should try there again, since the man you worked for is now in Pilsen."

"They won't take me back. I was arrested for stealing something there. I didn't do it, but nobody would listen."

"There are plenty of restaurants in town. Have you tried them?"

"I'll have to try the restaurants. You wouldn't have any money on you, would you? I'm all out of everything around here."

If he gave the man money, he'd soon be calling at their law office, asking for more. "No, I didn't bring any money with me. I don't have any to spare, anyway." He didn't know what more he could say, but he'd give it one more try. "Has it occurred to you that your country needs you? We're in bad shape now with the occupation. If you aren't concerned about your parents, think about Czechoslovakia. We need every citizen to be productive in some way."

"I am concerned about my parents and my country," he whined. "I just can't get a job." He looked as if he were near tears.

Anton stood. "I need to go now. Please think about what I've said." He left young Kopecky sitting there, looking helpless.

He felt sorry for old Mr. Kopecky, and he dreaded calling the man and telling him he hadn't done any good. It would have to be done, though, and he'd call when he got back to the office after seeing Eliska off.

A leisurely walk to the Café Slavia would get him there at just about the right time to meet Eliska. It had turned cloudy while he was in the house, and a chilly wind was blowing. He started to wish he had worn a jacket. By the time he reached the restaurant, a light rain was falling. The black Mercedes was parked outside, and through the fogged windows he could make out the same young German who had taken them to the party. The passenger seat was piled with suitcases, and the lid of the trunk was tied down—it wouldn't close because of the trunk and bags inside.

Eliska was already there, seated by one of the front windows. She looked lovely in a plum-colored suit with a matching hat. He leaned down and kissed her cheek. "I'm going to miss you so," she said.

"I'll miss you, too." He couldn't help thinking this was happening at the most opportune time, since he found himself becoming more attached to Tereza every day. It would mean a loss of opportunity to find out what was happening with her German friends, but there was nothing to be done about that.

The waiter came with soup. "I ordered for you. I know what you like."

He had to agree that she did. He wanted to ask whether she had been at his apartment last night, but he knew she would want to know where he'd been, and he couldn't think what to tell her. "What time does your train leave?"

"It leaves at three, but I should get there early. I have quite a few bags."

"I noticed. Have some arrangements been made to get you across the border?"

"My father-in-law will meet me with a car. He assures me there won't be a problem. They've been most generous."

And they'd undoubtedly be most generous with border guards. "I hope the rain stops before you get there."

"I was hoping to see you last night for one last fling. I went by your apartment, but I couldn't wait, because I still had a lot of packing to do. Where were you?"

"My aunt wasn't feeling well. I spent the night with her to make sure she was going to be okay."

"You're very thoughtful, as always. As I said in my note, Hans will be staying in my house. He'll look after the place while I'm gone."

"Do you think you'll be back in Prague someday?"

"Of course. As soon as the war ends, we'll move back here. You don't think I could leave you and my other friends forever, do you?"

If he survived the war, and more importantly, if Tereza survived, there wouldn't be a place for Eliska in his life. He couldn't say this now, however. They finished lunch, and he took care of the bill. The rain was coming down harder now, and they rushed to the car. The driver helped Eliska into the front seat, and Anton squeezed into the back with the suitcases. The young man drove them to the station, where Anton helped him unload the luggage and get it onto a porter's cart. Anton told the driver to go on; he would help the porter get the bags into Eliska's compartment and into the baggage compartment of the train. She fluttered around, trying to decide which ones she needed with her, but finally they were all sorted out. Anton kissed her goodbye in her compartment, and she promised to write him. She waved to him at the window as the train pulled away.

The rain was pouring down now, and he found a bench and sat in the station for a while. He had no umbrella, and it would be impossible to get a taxi in this downpour. He sat there wondering whether he should send a message through his contact about Eliska's leaving; that source of information drying up. He decided that he should. Of course the hostess at the party, Mrs. Horakova, might invite him to more functions, considering the fact that she knew Teta Adelka so well. Going to them would be the last thing he'd want to do, but he would have to make that decision later if she invited him.

The rain stopped suddenly, and he hurried through the wet streets to his office. He called Mr. Kopecky. "Sir, I saw your son today"

"How'd it go?"

"I'm afraid I wasn't able to do much good."

"He wouldn't listen to you?"

"Well, he did listen, at least. I told him about your concerns and encouraged him to find work. I hate to say this, but it appears he might be an alcoholic."

"I've reached that conclusion myself."

Anton could hear the sadness in the old man's tone. "How long has he been drinking that way?"

"Quite sometime. Years. I've talked to him about it. Nothing changed."

"Until he stops . . ."

"Yes, I'm afraid you're right. In any case, I do appreciate your seeing him and trying. I don't think there's anything else we can do for him."

Anton agreed and hung up. It was time to go home and code a message about Eliska's departure. Then he'd take whatever food Mrs. Svobodova left for him to Tereza's apartment.

#

They set the food aside and made love in Tereza's bed. He felt so grateful to somebody, something, maybe just to fate, that he had found her. He knew without any reservations that he was happy Eliska was gone. It was all about Tereza now. He held her tight for an hour, even though they both were famished.

"There's only one problem with sex," he said.

86

"What's that?" She sounded worried.

"It works up an appetite, and food isn't that easy to come by."

She laughed. "It's worth the misery of being hungry. Besides, I have a surprise. There's this young man in the supply room. I think he has a crush on me. He gave me a couple of oranges, and I brought them home. I didn't know whether I could get them past the searcher, but she didn't seem to notice. I just put them on a table in the room where we're searched. I picked them up and carried them out when I left."

So a young man had a crush on her already. This brought up a subject he'd been trying not to think about. She might feel the need to go to bed with a Nazi in order to obtain information. Should he tell her not to tell him about it if she did? He didn't want to talk about it now, and never would.

"Is everything okay?"

"I'm just hungry. My landlady left a potato dish of some kind. I think it has some cheese in it."

"I have a tiny bit of bread, too, and with the oranges, we'll have plenty."

"Let's eat, and then I need to go. I want to spend the nights with you, but I think my chances of getting out of your apartment without being seen are better this time of day than in the morning, when everyone's going to work."

They ate the potatoes and bread, leaving the oranges for dessert. When they were through they had the last of the tea. "Tell me about your day," Anton said.

"It was actually identical to yesterday, except for the oranges. I wonder if the woman who does the searching is one of us. It's not likely, though, because she's in a German uniform. Maybe she just feels bad because of the food shortages and ignored the oranges. Anyway, I still can't see how I'll ever get the camera into the palace."

"That's not for you to worry about. It'll be arranged." He kissed her and left her; he was feeling for the first time in his life the bittersweet longing all lovers feel at the moment of parting.

#

Anton stopped at the Tyn Church early the next morning to meet his contact and found that the contact also had a message for him. He accepted he newspaper that contained the message and took it home to decode it. Once deciphered, it instructed him to take Erik and Jakub to Pilsen on Saturday to meet a contact at the Hotel Continental. Anton would return to Prague alone; Erik and Jakub would remain in Pilsen. Erik would have to figure out how to deal with his parents.

Maybe he could tell them he had a job offer in Pilsen. Most likely the "job" had to do with what was planned for the Skoda Munitions Works. Anton had been trained to kill with a knife and with his hands, if necessary. A large, muscular man with a shaved head, a man of few words, had spent a day with him at a clearing in the woods near Benosov, showing him the fundamentals. He could still remember the bizarre contrast of the bird songs from the nearby trees as he concentrated on learning to thrust a knife into just the right spot to reach the heart.

Now, he supposed, it was Jakub and Erik's turn. What a pity that teenagers had to be relied on for this work. It was a reflection of the fragmented state of the resistance since the reprisals after the assassination of Heydrich. He wondered how much beer the young men would drink in a town famous for its beer, but decided they wouldn't have enough money to make it a serious problem.

They left early Saturday; he could get there and back the same day. Their meeting was scheduled for eleven in the morning in the hotel restaurant, where a man would ask if they were looking for work. Erik and Jakub would reply that they were and would leave with the contact.

They were stopped by soldiers at the edge of Prague. They showed their papers, and one of the soldiers, a tall, gangly youth, leaned down. "Where are you going?"

"We're going to Pilsen. We heard rumors that the hotels were hiring there, and we're looking for work."

That seemed to satisfy the soldier, and he waved them on. Cars were backing up behind them. "What are we going to be doing in Pilsen," Jakub asked.

"I don't know. I wasn't given that information. A contact will be waiting for us, and you'll find out eventually. I'm to leave you there and come back alone."

"Do you have any idea how long we'll be there?" Erik asked.

"I don't know that either."

"I told my parents I had a job offer, and I'd try to come home on weekends unless I had to work then. I tried to be vague about it. They're worried, as usual."

They arrived at the Continental near the main square in Pilsen. Anton found a parking place, and they went into the restaurant and ordered coffee. It was a few minutes before eleven. They drank the coffee slowly and waited. There were a few other people in the restaurant, but no one approached them. At eleven-fifteen, Anton was getting concerned. "We're leaving at eleven-thirty if no one shows up." If their contact had been detained by the Gestapo or SS, he might be telling them right now that he was to meet three men in the restaurant at the Continental.

Jakub looked grim. "This is disappointing. I was looking forward to taking part in something big for a change."

"I was, too." Erik said. The look on his face said something different, however; he would be glad to go home to the safety of the family farm.

"Okay, we're leaving." The hands on Anton's watch showed eleven-thirty. They got up and he paid for the coffee. As they walked to the car, they could see a Gestapo officer coming down the street toward them. "Don't rush," Anton said. "Just take it easy and get into the car slowly. Jakub, you get behind the wheel."

Jakub didn't question this but did as he was told. Erik got in the backseat. The officer pulled out his Luger as he approached them. Anton took his gun from under the dash and covered it with a map they had used to find the hotel. The officer got in the backseat with Erik and pointed the pistol at his head. Erik's face was white. "Turn the car around. We need to go to headquarters to check your papers."

If the contact had revealed their plans, wouldn't they have sent officers in cars for them? What was this man doing?

Anton suspected he had taken a fancy to the Citroen Rosalie, old as it was, and was determined to dispose of them one way or another so he could have the car. But if this were the case, why hadn't their contact shown up? Why couldn't their work be simple?

Anton had the cyanide pill in his pocket, but he didn't think the teenagers had one. His contact had given him one early on, and Anton had gotten the impression that this wasn't the usual thing for members of the resistance.

Could he shoot the officer without Erik getting shot in the process? They were all dead anyway, unless he did something. Jakub started the car. Anton could see that his hands were shaking. "Go down here and turn left on the next street," the officer said.

They were heading away from Gestapo headquarters. He was going to take them out in the country and shoot them. If Anton showed his gun, Erik would be dead immediately, he was sure of that. They were on the next street now, and traffic was light. Anton lifted the gun and fired a shot through the seat back. The officer had a stunned look on his face when the bullet struck him in the chest. Erik had the presence of mind to grab the hand holding the pistol and point it toward the roof of the car. The gun went off as the officer slumped forward.

Anton's ears were ringing. He could see a man walking down the street turning to look at them—it was obvious he was curious about the sound of gunshots but wary of appearing to be too curious.

"Drive slowly, Jakub. Erik, prop him up and get his jacket off." He took off his shirt. Fortunately he had worn an undershirt. "Put this on him, and then lean him back against the seat. Maybe it'll look like he's sleeping. Not so fast, Jakub. We need to get out of here without being stopped. Good job, Erik. Just put his jacket on the floor and push it back under the seat."

No one said anything till they reached the edge of Pilsen. "Would you rather I'd drive?" Anton asked.

"I'm okay. What are we going to do with him?"

"There's a road ahead that cuts over to Kladno. We'll take it. It's a country road, and we'll find a place to pull off where we can drag his body into the woods. We'll take all his clothes off. I want to keep everything. We won't leave any identifying items on him. By the time the animals in the woods get through, there won't be much left but bones."

Erik had finished buttoning Anton's shirt, and blood was seeping through the front. "What are you going to do with his things? It won't be safe to keep them."

"I'll find a place. They could be useful in the future."

Jakub turned on the road to Kladno, and they were immediately surrounded by woods. "If you see a dirt road leading off this, preferably one that doesn't lead to a house, turn in."

They had gone almost five miles before they came to such a road. It led a short distance into the forest and stopped at a clearing where someone had been cutting firewood. "Okay, let's get his clothes off. Then we'll drag him farther into the woods. First we'll put all his things in the trunk." They took his identification, his wallet, his wedding ring, and all his clothes and shoes. They were elated to have the pistol, and Jakub asked Anton to let him keep it. Anton refused. He bundled everything up in the trunk, careful that the blood from the jacket and his shirt not spread to anything else, and covered it with some rags that had been used to wash the car in some long-ago time when car washing had been the thing to do.

The man's body looked pathetic, but Anton couldn't bring himself to feel sympathy or remorse for the shooting. After all, he was a member of the Gestapo. Erik took one arm and Anton the other, and they dragged him deep into the woods. Jakub stayed with the car with the excuse that he needed to urinate if anyone came along. They couldn't think of a way to explain the bullet holes except that they had been in the car when his friend bought it.

All was quiet when they returned to the car. "I'll drive now," Anton said. "I know the way."

"What are we going to do if we get stopped?" Erik asked. "What if they search the trunk?"

"We're all dead," Anton said. "I think it's worth the risk. That uniform could be invaluable in getting someone out of the country."

"What if they notice the bullet holes?"

"I bought the car from my aunt. She had many lovers, and one shot another once after a heated argument in the car. His first shot was deflected by my aunt, and it went through the roof. He pushed her aside and shot the man in the backseat through the front seat, since the lover in the backseat was reaching over, trying to choke him. Does that sound believable?"

"No. Besides, there's a smell of gunpowder and blood in the car."

"Maybe it'll air out by the time we get to town. Keep the windows down."

They were back on the road to Kladno now, and Anton shifted into high gear. Teta Adelka would be mortified if she knew of the story Anton had thought up, but it was all he could come up with. She was such a modest maiden lady, but maybe she looked back on her life and wished for some such excitement.

They reached Kladno and drove through town with no problems. Anton glanced at Erik in the rearview mirror now and then, and he looked as grim and nervous as one teenager could look. Jakub was looking jaunty beside Anton, almost as if he were hoping for a confrontation. Anton would drop Erik off beside the lane that led to his house before they got to Prague. Now if Jakub would just be sensible if they were stopped, they might make it.

"You'll have to tell your parents that the job didn't work out. They had given it to someone else when you got there."

"That's what I'm going to tell them. I hope they don't send us out on any more of these assignments."

"It's possible they will once they find out what happened to our contact."

Erik looked miserable at the mention of the contact. "He's probably at Gestapo headquarters spilling his guts about how he was supposed to meet us and where he was supposed to meet us."

"He may be, but he wouldn't have our names or know where we're from." This was probably true, but there could be another problem—maybe someone had seen the officer pull his gun and get in the car with them. The Rosalie was easily identifiable, but there was no need to discuss all this with Erik and Jakub now.

"What about the man you shot? Did they send him to intercept us?"

"I don't think so. If the contact had told them about our meeting, they would have sent a swarm of cars to the Continental. I think that man wanted the car. The way he was directing us to drive was away from their headquarters."

"How do you know where their headquarters is?"

"I came here to a friend's wedding just after the occupation started. I asked him about it, and drove by there to check it out."

Jakub looked at him. "Were you involved with the resistance then?"

"Yes. But don't ask me any more." He was concerned Jakub might ask how he was recruited, and he didn't want to go into detail. He had been at work one day early in the occupation when a man appeared and asked to see him about making a will. When he was seated in Anton's office, the man asked whether he would be interested in helping Czechoslovakia against the Nazis.

"Why did you choose me?" Anton asked.

"You're young and single, you live alone, and you graduated near the top of your class in law school, so you're obviously bright. In addition, you're involved with a woman who has contacts among the Germans. In fact, she's married to a German. She could be a source of information that would be useful."

They certainly knew a lot about him. He wanted to think it over. "I'll make up a will for you. Come back in a week and I'll give you the answer. What's your name?"

"For the will? Put it in the name Jan Neruda."

Anton smiled. "Like the poet? Okay. What assets do you want to include in the will?"

"Only my house. That's my only asset. I have no relatives, so I want to leave it to the city of Prague. It's located at 100 Nerudova Street."

"This will be very simple. Come back in a week and it'll be ready, along with my answer."

"If you're concerned about your aunt, we'll do all we can to protect her if you become involved."

Obviously, the man was an admirer of Jan Neruda, and maybe he knew Anton was also. That was probably one more thing they knew about him. They knew about Teta Adelka, too. Anton was concerned not only about her, but also about his own survival. But how worthwhile would his life be if the occupation kept on for years? He wrote the will in a few minutes; the decision to join the resistance took somewhat longer.

Before the week was over, he knew he had to do it. It would be something, a minor strike against the Nazis now inhabiting his beloved Prague. If it got them out even a week sooner, it would be worth it. The man using Jan Neruda as an alias came back, and Anton told him he wanted to be involved. The man had explained the system of telephone signals to him—he knew Anton's phone number, also—and said he'd be in touch. He was the man who now was Anton's contact at the Our Lady of Victory Church, the Tyn Church, and the Café Slavia.

#

They dropped Erik off near his house and continued toward Prague. Anton turned to Jakub. "I'm going to drop you off this side of town. You'll have to walk a few miles, but you'll be safer."

"I'm going with you. If we go down, we go down together."

Anton stopped the car on the side of the road. "Get out."

"No. I'm going with you."

"They need you. We can't afford to lose any more people than have already been lost. If I don't make it, you carry on. Erik needs a lot of help and encouragement. He'd be lost without you."

This seemed to convince him, and Jakub got out. He reached in his pocket and took out a rosary, which he handed to Anton. "For protection. For luck." He walked away, and Anton drove on alone.

CHAPTER TWELVE

The city was quiet, with no roadblocks. Anton put the Rosalie in the garage and went to his apartment. He'd return to the car after dark with a paper bag for carrying the Gestapo uniform and the other items they'd salvaged. He sat down at the kitchen table and coded a message asking for information about the contact who failed to appear. It was possible his contact didn't know what happened and was thinking Erik and Jakub were in Pilsen, ready to tackle a mission, so this would alert him. He also asked about a body shop that could be trusted to repair the Rosalie with no questions asked and the name of a tailor that could be trusted for reweaving the Gestapo uniform where the bullet had penetrated. Fortunately, it was only the front of the jacket that was damaged. The bullet had lodged somewhere inside the man.

He signaled his contact for a meeting at Café Slavia at eight in the morning. They needed to meet at a place where they could talk, like old friends meeting for coffee. He was desperate to find out what happened to the contact in Pilsen, and whether they'd been betrayed and the Gestapo would be kicking in his door by tomorrow.

He wouldn't see Tereza this afternoon, just in case he had somehow been identified. He thought about the time Erik had showed up at her apartment and said he'd found it by following Anton. Anton hadn't noticed that he was being followed; this was one covert skill he hadn't acquired yet. He was afraid now that someone could follow him to Tereza's apartment and he wouldn't discover he was being followed until too late. He told her not to call him except in emergencies, so he hoped she would know he was okay and just couldn't make it.

Mrs. Svobodova pecked on his door and delivered a bit of what they considered goulash these days—it contained virtually no meat. He ate it and still felt hungry, but it would have to do. It was still an hour till full dark, so he took down a book of Jan Neruda's poems, *Cemetery Flowers.* It had been a while since he had read anything by the poet, but thinking of his contact reminded him of one of his favorite books.

When darkness finally fell, he took a large paper bag from his pantry and went to the garage. He put the officer's gun in the bottom of the bag, followed by the boots and the man's identity papers, and then the clothes. He took the things upstairs and washed the blood, which had started to dry, out of the gray jacket. He took down his suitcase, a scarred brown leather case that reminded him of happier times, and put everything in it but the jacket. That he hung in the bathroom to dry, and then sat down with the dead man's identification papers. His name was Erich Stossel, and he was from Munich.

Anton finished going through the documents and photos that undoubtedly were of the man's wife and son. He went to bed with the hope that his door wouldn't be broken down in the middle of the night.

#

A chilly drizzle was falling. He put on a trench coat and carried his umbrella, hoping this would make him look more like a traveler as he carried the suitcase to the train station. He had the book of Neruda poems in the pocket of his coat with the coded message folded between pages. The streets were busy with people going to work, and he had no opportunity to look around to see if he was being followed. He simply hurried down the crowded street. At the station, he found an empty locker and put his suitcase in it.

He'd given some thought to the problem of what to do with the key, but hadn't come up with a perfect solution. A flowerpot with a dead geranium in it stood at the entrance to Mrs. Svobodova's bakery, and he had considered pushing the key into the dirt in the pot, but if the landlady decided to transplant something, that could be a problem. He'd carry it with him for the moment until a better solution was found.

And in the end, his hiding place in the Rosalie probably would have to hold the key also.

He walked to the Café Slavia, where his contact was waiting with a cup of coffee. Anton ordered coffee and a roll, which was available that morning, and the waiter went away. "I'm concerned about the Pilsen contact. Do you know what happened?"

"He was picked up. He didn't know your names or where you live. Maybe he had the opportunity to take the capsule before they got to headquarters. Most unfortunate. Everything is on hold for now."

The waiter came with Anton's coffee and the roll. There was no butter, just the roll. Anton took small bites and chewed it slowly. He was so hungry, he knew it would make him sick if he wolfed it down. "It's important I get an answer as soon as possible," he said. He had placed the trench coat over the back of the chair next to him. He took the book from the pocket and handed it to the contact. "I thought you might enjoy this book of Neruda's poems. It's a loan, not a gift. I enjoy his work very much myself."

The man who had called himself Jan Neruda slipped the book into the pocket of his jacket. "Neruda's work is banned, you know."

"I know, but no one is watching. We can't live our entire lives hiding behind our window curtains, afraid to go out into the world and do anything."

"I'll look forward to reading these. This is one of his books that I don't have." He finished his coffee and went out into the drizzle.

Anton sat at the table a while longer, taking his time with the coffee, which was a little stronger than usual. He'd spend the day at his office today, taking care of business, and maybe he could find a place there to hide the locker key, which was in his pants pocket. He finished his coffee, paid his bill, and walked out the door.

He immediately heard shouting from down the street, and he could see two SS officers wrestling with a civilian. They pushed the man to the sidewalk, and one of the officers drew out his pistol and shot the man three times. He kicked the body off the sidewalk and into the gutter, and they walked away.

Anton was going in that direction, and he walked slowly, letting the SS officers get farther down the street. As he approached the body, he thought the man looked familiar. He was staring at the sky with eyes wide open and the steady drizzle wetting his face. Then Anton realized it was Mr. Kopecky's son. He felt sick, thinking about the discussion he'd had with young Kopecky. He'd told him his country needed him, that it was his duty to straighten out his life and do something for Czechoslovakia. Had his lecture prompted the man to attack the SS officers? He'd never know exactly what happened, since this sort of thing never made the papers.

He felt the need to see Mr. Kopecky in person to explain what he'd seen, and he walked to the old man's house before going to the office. Mr. Kopecky came to the door with his cane. "Come in, Mr. Janak. The wife can get you some coffee."

"Thanks, Mr. Kopecky, but I've just had coffee. I'm afraid I have some very bad news for you. Your son has been killed by the SS. I saw it happen as I was coming down the street."

Mr. Kopecky's face turned a sickly shade of gray, and he sat down in his rocker. Mrs. Kopecky came from the kitchen. She had heard what Anton said; she was sobbing. "How did it happen?" Mr. Kopecky asked.

"I had met a friend at the Café Slavia. I was just coming out when I heard shouting, and your son was struggling with two SS officers. They shoved him down, and one of them drew his pistol and fired three times. His body is lying on the edge of the street, just down from the restaurant."

"I don't know what would provoke him to do such a thing."

"I hope it wasn't something I said to him the other day. I told him he needed to get his life straightened out and do the best he could for Czechoslovakia. I hope this didn't prompt him . . ."

"It wasn't your fault. Only a madman would see that as a reason to confront the SS."

"Anyway, I'm terribly sorry it happened. Is there anything I can do for you?"

Tears began running down Mr. Kopecky's cheeks. His wife had disappeared into the adjoining room and still could be heard sobbing. "I'm completely out of money. I don't even have enough to bury him. I can stop the rent on his apartment, and maybe we'll be able to have more food now."

"I'll call the mortuary. I'll take care of it. You've been a good client, and I want to do that for you and Mrs. Kopecky. I'll tell the funeral director to call you about arrangements."

Mr. Kopecky was crying in earnest now. He grabbed Anton's hand and held on to it. "You're a good man. I hope I can repay you some day, in some way."

"That won't be necessary. Don't even consider it." Anton went on to his office. The drizzle had stopped, but it was still cloudy and chilly. He called the mortuary near his office right away and arranged for the body to be picked up; he also made arrangements to pay them for their services. He liked old Mr. Kopecky, and he couldn't bear the idea of his son being shuffled off to a pauper's grave as an unknown.

He had just finished the call when Josef came in. "A young man came in a while ago, looking for you. He was tall and skinny, looked about twenty. He didn't say what he wanted. He said he just dropped in to say hello, that he knew you from the neighborhood."

Tall and skinny, about twenty. It sounded like Jakub. He knew not to come to the office unless it was something important. Anton decided he'd go to lunch at the Kolkovna and sit at one of Jakub's tables. Maybe they'd have a chance to talk. "Thanks. I think I know who it was. I'll check with him later." He finished up the work on his desk and took a letter to Martina for typing.

"Did you get a chance to see the young man who came by?" she asked.

"No, but I'll see him later. Has the mail come in today?"

"Not yet. I'll put yours on your desk when it comes."

He left his trench coat hanging in his office and left for the restaurant. The sun was breaking through the clouds now, and it promised to be a better afternoon. He still couldn't think of a good place for the locker key. Maybe he'd have to put it under the dashboard of the Rosalie with the gun and camera. After all, any of these items would be incriminating if the Nazis became suspicious of him, so he might as well have everything together. And he'd have to think of another place to keep them if a suitable body shop was available for fixing the car. And if a body shop wasn't available—well, that would be just one more bridge to cross when he came to it.

He reached the Kolkovna and sat in a remote corner, part of Jakub's section. The place was swarming with Germans, but they were sitting toward the front of the restaurant. Jakub came to his table, pad and pencil in hand. "Erik came here this morning. He said a body was found in that barn where you took Tereza after she landed in the tree."

He had told Erik not to come to town again unless he was told to do so, and he didn't see this as a reason for him to come. After all, neither Erik nor Jakub knew that he and Tereza had been back in that barn and that she had killed a man there. "Did you come to my office, or was it him?"

"He said he went to your office, and you weren't there. The police asked him to identify the body. He told them it was the man who owned the farm next to theirs. He wasn't living there, but came by now and then to check on things."

"Was it the SS or Gestapo?"

"He said they were Czech. He wasn't sure what kind of police they were. He said it looked like the man had been killed with a pitchfork. He'd been there a while from the looks of things. I need to take your order. My boss is getting suspicious."

"Just bring me some food. Whatever you have. I'm starving. Bring a glass of milk, too, if you have it."

Jakub rolled his eyes. "You're a dreamer, Anton. I'll bring coffee."

CHAPTER THIRTEEN

Tereza went to the cart room to get her cleaning supplies. She felt in the box of rags, and the camera was there, buried at the bottom, as Anton had said it would be. Things happened mysteriously, but that was the way it should be. She didn't want to know how they happened. If they caught her before she had a chance to take the cyanide capsule, betraying others was the last thing she wanted to do. And she hoped she could endure endless torture before she'd betray Anton. The capsule was there too, sealed in a small envelope beside the camera.

Now if she could just find something to photograph. The drawers in the desks of the rooms she cleaned were locked; she had checked that out already. Maybe someone would leave something on a desk, or maybe she'd have a chance at something that was being mimeographed.

She started with the supply room. Will was there, running off copies of something. "Good morning, Will."

"Good morning. I have a rush job this morning for somebody important." He looked as if he hoped to impress Tereza with his connection to one of the officers on the upper floors.

"I'm sure there are a lot of important people upstairs." She was fishing.

"It's for Reichsprotektor Daluege. Don't say I told you about it. I don't want to get in trouble."

"I wouldn't say a word." But she would take photos given the chance. Something from the big man himself.

"I have to deliver these copies. I'll be back before you're done cleaning. I'll bring you something to eat if I can."

He went off with his copies, leaving the stencil on the drum of the machine. Tereza ran off another copy, folded it, and put it in the bottom of her rag box with the camera and cyanide capsule. She was cleaning the supply shelves when he returned with two small pieces of apple strudel.

"Thanks. I'm hungry. I didn't have anything for breakfast." It was the truth. Maybe if she let Will know frequently that she didn't have much to eat, he would supply as much as he could get his hands on. The strudel was delicious, and he insisted she eat both pieces after telling him she'd had no breakfast. She felt sorry for him, but she couldn't let this interfere with taking advantage of the information and food he could furnish.

"Would you like to go out with me some evening? We could go to a movie or the theater."

She had been expecting this. She'd have to weigh whether it would be advantageous for her work against the problems it could cause. She dreaded the thought of being hated by her fellow workers for consorting with the enemy, and she had no doubt they'd find out, sooner or later. "I don't know if that's appropriate, Will. After all, you're my employer in a way." Stall for now.

He looked uncomfortable at being rejected and busied himself with taking the stencil from the mimeograph machine. He laid it out to dry beside the machine. She wanted to ask what happened to the stencils once the project was printed, but thought this might arouse his suspicions. Maybe if she took long enough with her dusting, she'd find out.

He left with a stack of supplies, and she continued dusting, slowly. When he came back, he took the stencil and left with it. They obviously had a storage area for the stencils somewhere in the building. The Germans were meticulous record-keepers and never threw anything away, this she had learned in training. The challenge was to find as many documents as she could and photograph them.

She finished in the supply room and moved on to the other offices. Most of them were occupied, but she cleaned as best she could. In one vacant room a note had been left on the desk—"Call me. Richard." This was the only piece of paper she found in any of the offices, although all of the workers had something on their desks—family photos, inkwells, and pens. Getting helpful information was going to be a slow process, she could see, and a lot would depend on carelessness, which was not a common German trait.

She finished early, put her cart away, and went to Olga to see if there was something more she should do until four o'clock. "Go up to the next floor—actually, I'd better go with you and show you the room," Olga said. "Colonel Schwann wants someone to set things up for a meeting. I'd better help you do it. The meeting's scheduled to start in a half hour."

They went upstairs to a large room with a long table in the center. A number of chairs were lined against the wall. "They need twelve chairs arranged around the table," Olga said, and they began carrying chairs to the table, planning to put five on each side and one on each end.

Tereza was aware of someone standing in the doorway, watching them. She glanced over and saw that it was a tall man with a colonel's insignia on his gray uniform. He was staring directly at her. "What's your name?"

"Tereza Valentova."

He smiled. "A lovely name. How long have you worked here?"

She continued moving chairs. "This is my second week."

"You speak German well. Where did you learn German?"

"I grew up in the Sudetenland. My mother was German."

"And you're on the cleaning crew. I think you'd be more useful in some other line of work."

Her greatest fear was that they'd want to use her as a translator when Czech prisoners were being tortured for information. "I'm happy with my job."

He asked them to set out coffee cups and bring a large coffeemaker to the sideboard at the end of the room. A private came in with a tray of pastries and set it beside the coffeemaker. How she'd love to stuff a dozen of those in a bag to take home and share with Anton.

She and Olga went back downstairs, and Tereza got in line to be searched. Natalie got in line behind her. "Did you hear about Pavlina?" she whispered.

"No. Isn't she the one who was in line when we were talking the other day?"

"Yes. I heard she'd been stealing office supplies and selling them on the black market. It's just a rumor. Anyway, they took her away."

"What will happen to her?"

The guard was scowling at them. "I don't know, but I'm sure it's nothing good," Natalie said.

Tereza went in to be searched. The thought of Pavlina being taken away to some unknown fate gave her the chills. She hadn't been near her cyanide capsule when she and Olga went to the room upstairs. Maybe she should carry it in her bra when she was away from the cart. That meant she'd have to return downstairs to the cart before leaving, something that might be regarded as suspicious. The covert life wasn't something that was all tied up in a neat little bundle, as she'd imagined at Catoctin Mountain Park. The ties on that bundle were constantly popping loose in an unruly fashion.

#

She stopped at her favorite store, which was just two blocks from her apartment. The store owner, a plump, pleasant man with a crown of blonde hair surrounding a bald spot, had gotten to know her. He sometimes saved things for her, since she came in almost every evening. She bought bread and a little cheese, and he brought a pear from under the counter. Anton would be pleased. She gave him her coupons, paid him, and went home.

Anton came in shortly. He had more bread, and he put it with hers. They'd be eating plenty of bread this evening. "I missed you last night," she said.

"I missed you, too. There will be times when I can't make it. Just know I'll always try to be here."

She began unbuttoning his shirt. "I understand."

"Let's take a shower," he said. They made love with warm water streaming and splashing over them, laughing at the awkwardness of it.

CHAPTER FOURTEEN

He stayed at his apartment past ten o'clock the next morning, hoping the phone would ring with an invitation to a meeting. He was eager for an answer to his questions of the day before. He felt he must leave to put in an appearance at the office, and he had just reached the bottom of the stairs when he heard the phone. Three o'clock this afternoon, Our Lady of Victory Church.

He had put the locker key in the Rosalie last night. The key and the gun would both have to go somewhere in his room if a trustworthy body shop was available to fix the bullet holes. The Gestapo jacket had been dry last night, with barely a trace of the blood stain still visible, and he wrapped it in brown paper and tied it with a string. It now rested on the high shelf in his closet.

He walked to work, stopping to look in a shop window now and then to see if he was being followed. He'd been practicing this now, since he found out Erik followed him from his office to Tereza's apartment, and he hadn't noticed. No one was there today, just the usual pedestrians coming and going as he stood in front of the windows.

#

He left the office at two because he wanted to enjoy what was probably one of the last pleasant afternoons of the fall. He'd linger on the Charles Bridge and watch the Vltava flow by. Sometimes he could almost pretend that life was normal.

Karel and Vaclav were in the reception area, flirting with Martina. "Leaving early again?" Vaclav said.

"I have business to take care of." Anton was carrying his briefcase.

Vaclav didn't say anything more, just smirked. Anton wondered just what would happen if either of the two were

107

pressed for information about him. Josef had been his best friend since college, and he could be trusted. Of the other two, he wasn't sure. Maybe they thought he was seeing a lady friend, and he'd tried to foster that opinion. He was sure they knew Eliska had stopped divorce proceedings and gone to Germany. They probably knew he had gone to a party where German officers were present. Maybe they thought he was in cahoots with the Germans. God only knew what they thought, but he was afraid to ask

He walked slowly and spent fifteen minutes on the bridge. A young couple walked by, laughing, and he thought of his own youthful romances when Czechoslovakia was free, a republic. That time would come again.

He arrived early at the church, and he sat in a pew in the center of the building. An elderly woman in a black scarf was kneeling in a pew at the front—she was the only one present. The place always gave him a feeling of peace, even though he was a skeptic. He wondered again about Tereza. Was she a believer? If so, he was sure she was Catholic. They would marry after the war, he was sure of that, and she probably would insist on being married in the church. He wouldn't object; he had been raised in it. His doubts had come later.

The contact came in and sat beside him. He laid the book of poems on the seat, and then got up and walked farther up the center aisle to another pew. He knelt and bowed his head. Anton put the book in his briefcase and left the church. It was too nice a day to go directly home, so he stopped at the Slavia for coffee. He sat by the windows at the front where he could see the river.

He had almost finished his coffee when a woman approached his table. "May I join you?"

"Certainly." He stood and held a chair for her.

"Aren't you Anton Janak?"

"Yes." He couldn't help staring at her. She had red hair, unusual for a Czech, and blue eyes. She had one of those placid, perfect faces that gave no clue as to what was going on inside her head. Her figure was just as perfect. If only the partners could see him now, they'd have no doubts about how he was spending his time away from the office.

"I'm Maria Dvorakova. I'm in need of legal assistance."

Why hadn't she come into the office, instead of approaching him here in the Slavia? "What sort of assistance do you need?"

"My husband died during a protest just prior to the German invasion. Now my in-laws are threatening to cheat me out of my inheritance, even though his will is plain enough. He left everything to me."

He finished his coffee. "Let's go to my office." This would give the partners fuel for gossip and speculation. "Do you have the will with you?"

"Yes. It's in my purse."

She put her hand through his arm as they went toward the office. In her high heels, she was nearly as tall as he was. She held his arm right on through the building. Fortunately, his space was at the back, and they'd pass the other partners on the way through. And fortunately everyone was still there, including Martina, who loved to gossip. Now Maria Dvorakova was seated at his desk.

"May I see the will?"

She handed it to him, and he read through it. "This seems straight-forward enough. Why would your in-laws think they could challenge it?"

"They say I don't deserve his money." She smiled. "I had an affair with my husband's cousin. I tried to be discreet, but someone found out, and the family has been in an uproar ever since. They can't take my inheritance, can they?"

"Not legally. There's quite a bit of property involved here. I think my first move should be to speak to them."

"They won't be receptive to any talk. They've hired a lawyer, too. They're especially upset because of the country estate. My husband inherited it from an uncle who never married, and I want to sell it. I can't stand the thought of living in the country. I love Prague, and I intend to stay here. That house and land need the attention of a live-in owner, and I don't intend to be that."

"I'll try reasoning with them." He gave the will back to her. "Why did you choose me to represent you?"

"Why, because of Eliska, of course. She said you're the best-looking attorney in Prague."

"You know Eliska?"

"She's my best friend. She told me to look after Hans while she's gone."

"You know Hans, too?"

"Yes, and that's something else my in-laws are upset about. They're fanatics, and just because I know a couple of Germans, they hate me."

"Would you be willing to sell the country place to them?"

"I'd rather not, now that they've been so mean to me."

"I'll try talking to them. It can't hurt."

Now she was smiling again. "Are you invited to Mrs. Horakova's party Saturday?"

"No, I haven't been invited."

"That's too bad. I was looking forward to dancing with you."

He took out a pad and pen. "Give me your address and phone number, and also the information for your in-laws. I'll be in touch."

"Soon, I hope."

He walked with her to the reception area, back past all the partners. Martina handed him an envelope. "A man delivered this. He said he's Mrs. Horakova's butler."

"Then you are invited to the party!" Maria kissed his cheek in front of a wide-eyed Martina. "I'll see you Saturday night."

Now let them gossip about this. He went back to his office. Karel pecked on his doorjamb. "Who the devil was that?"

"Just a client."

"Damn, you get all the good-looking ones. What's her name?"

"Maria Dvorakova."

"What's her problem?"

"Just a complication with a will."

"Her parents?"

"No, her deceased husband."

"She's a widow then." Karel was practically licking his chops.

"You're married, remember?"

110

"Did you have to remind me?"

Somewhere a phone was ringing. Anton chuckled. "That's probably your wife calling right now."

He left the office and walked to his apartment. He decoded the message the contact had passed to him in the Neruda poetry book. He was disappointed with the first phrase he saw—No body shop. The second part was more encouraging: Tailor Bedrich Hrabe corner Husova and Karlova. So, not too far, near the Klementinum. At least he could get rid of the Gestapo jacket. It was too late today, but he'd take it tomorrow before going to work.

He decided to do what he could to camouflage the damage to the car before going to Tereza's. If he worked in the garage after dark he'd need a flashlight, and the light would show through the windows, so best to do it while he could use the natural light. He found some duct tape and an old paint brush in the cabinet under the sink. In the garage, he took down a paint can from a shelf. It contained a bit of the paint he had used to change the color of the Rosalie to black.

He found his hammer and used it to tap the ragged edge of the hole in the roof until it was flush with the top of the car. Then he placed a piece of duct tape over the hole and coated that with black paint. Not bad in the dim garage, and he hoped it wouldn't be too noticeable in bright sunlight. The hole in the inside roof would have to remain, unless he could find a tape that would match the upholstery. If he found such a tape, it would also match the passenger seat with bullet holes in the front and back. In the meantime he'd find a blanket somewhere and throw it over the front seat to cover the damage. He had only one blanket, and he'd need that with winter coming on.

He was later than usual going to Tereza's, so he took the jar of soup Mrs. Svobodova left while he was in the garage and carried it in the knapsack to Tereza's apartment. She was waiting for him with a loaf of bread. "I was afraid you weren't coming."

"Sorry I'm late. I had a project that couldn't wait. Let's go to bed and make up for lost time."

#

It was a few minutes past curfew when he arrived back at his apartment, but no one seemed to notice. He saw several people hurrying to make it home in time. He'd forgotten the invitation from Mrs. Horakova, and it was still lying there on his table, unopened. It was for the party Saturday night, and the hostess had written a note on the side. "Mr. Janak, I don't have your home address. The driver will pick you up at your office at eight-thirty p.m. Saturday."

He considered letting her know that he couldn't come. He was fairly sure Maria was ready and willing to go to bed with him anytime, anywhere. Before Tereza, he would have been just as willing to go to bed with her. But he was truly in love for the first time in his life. He had no interest in going to bed with anyone but Tereza. But it was his duty to get as much information as possible and funnel it through his contact, so he had to go. He called her R.S.V.P. phone number and advised the maid that he'd be able to attend.

#

A shirt without a button was what he needed. Going to a tailor shop with a briefcase didn't look natural, but if he were carrying a shirt on a hanger, he wouldn't arouse any suspicion. He looked through his shirts and found one he'd shuffled aside because it had a button missing. It was slightly faded and worn to the soft and comfortable stage. He put the Gestapo jacket, still wrapped in paper and tied with string, in his briefcase. He felt a little silly carrying a shirt on a hanger through town, but if that's what it took, that's what he'd do.

Bedrich Hrabe was a small man with a large mustache and gold-rimmed glasses. He was cutting fabric at a table at the back of the shop. He put down his scissors. "May I help you?"

"I have two items that need some work. The first is a shirt with a button missing. Do you have a button that would match?"

The tailor's look said anyone ought to know how to sew on a button. "I'm sure I do."

Anton opened the briefcase and took out the bundle. "This is a jacket with a hole in the front. Can you reweave it?"

"I'll have to see it to know for sure." He untied the string, opened the paper, and held the jacket up. He looked at Anton

112

for what seemed like a long time. "I believe I can mend it. It won't be perfect, but it won't be terribly noticeable."

"There's also a faint stain. Can you do anything about that?"

"I'll see what I can do."

"When can I pick up the garments?"

"Give me a week. I'm working on a rush order for a wedding. I need your name." He now had a pen poised over a slip.

"Call me Hans." Anton hadn't been thinking about being asked his name, and he answered on the spur of the moment.

"What's your phone number?"

"I don't have a phone. I'll come back in a week."

"I'll try to have it ready by then." He wrapped the jacket in the paper again and tied it with the string. He started toward the back of the shop, and Anton left.

He had considered phoning Maria Dvorakova's in-laws to arrange to see them, but he decided they might refuse to see him if he did that. It would be better to just show up at their door and introduce himself. He'd go by there now before going to the office.

Their house wasn't far from Teta Adelka's, so he'd stop in and see her, too. He found the address Maria had given him and knocked on the door. A maid answered, and he gave her his name and asked to see Mr. Dvorak. She showed him into a library and asked him to wait. Mr. Dvorak appeared shortly, and Anton stood and extended his hand. "I'm Anton Janak. I've been retained to represent Maria Dvorakova in the matter of her husband's will."

Mr. Dvorak was a thoughtful, unassuming-looking man. He shook Anton's hand. "Please have a seat. Would you like coffee?"

The invitation was a surprise. "Yes, please. That would be a pleasure."

He rang a bell for the maid and asked her to bring coffee. "Mrs. Dvorakova is shopping now and won't be back for hours, but I can speak for both of us. We're determined Maria won't be able to profit from our son's death. We begged him not to marry her, but he always was headstrong. She's stolen from us and spent so much money that we had to bail them out several times. Now she's determined to sell my brother's estate in the country. All this, and the numerous affairs she's had have been too much."

"I can understand your frustration, but the will seems to be clear. I don't see how you can dispute it. Would you be willing to buy your brother's estate if she's willing to sell it?"

"I refuse to give the woman another cent, even to buy the property."

The maid appeared with a tray that held two cups of coffee, an urn with more, and a plate with two kolaches. "Please help yourself to those," the host said. "I don't eat them."

Anton did help himself, gladly. The coffee was decent, too. Mr. Dvorak was an unusually gracious host, considering the circumstances. "The kolaches are delicious," he said.

"Our cook makes those when she can get all the ingredients, which isn't too often these days. How's your law firm doing with this nasty occupation in place?"

"We're making it. I share an office with three other attorneys, and we manage to pay the rent and utility bills with a little left over." Anton picked up the second kolache. "You have quite a fascinating library here."

"We enjoy it. My wife and I are both readers." He refilled both their cups from the urn. "Did you say your name's Janak?"

"Yes, Anton Janak."

"Are you related to Miss Adelka Janakova?"

"She's my aunt. I'll be on my way to see her when I leave here. Do you know her?"

"Yes, we go to the same church. Have for years. Give her my regards. She's a fine lady."

Half the people in town knew Teta Adelka and seemed to give him their stamp of approval because of it. "I certainly will. I'm sure she'll be glad to hear from you." Anton had now finished off the second kolache. "I must be on my way. I appreciate your hospitality." He shook Mr. Dvorak's hand again, and the elderly man walked with him to the door. He obviously felt there was nothing more to be said about his son's estate.

The meeting wasn't at all what Anton had expected. He had anticipated hostility and probably a refusal to talk to him once he made his purpose known. The Dvoraks obviously were well-to-do, with a maid, a cook, and a wife spending the day shopping. Their house was impressive, too. Mr. Dvorak was a puzzle.

Anton walked on to Teta Adelka's house and knocked on the door. She answered, explaining that Zita was shopping. Zita was "shopping" in an alley where vendors sold produce stashed under their coats, Anton imagined. But whatever it took to keep his aunt eating was fine with him. He kissed her cheek. "I've just been talking with Mr. Dvorak. He sends his regards."

"You were talking with Mr. Dvorak?"

"Yes. It involves a case. I can't talk about it."

"I'm sure it involves that daughter-in-law of theirs. The whole church is buzzing about her behavior."

Anton laughed. "You mean all you church-goers are gossips?"

"Don't be impertinent, young man. It's just that the Dvoraks are wonderful people, and we all feel sorry for them."

"I apologize. How is everything going here? Are you getting enough to eat?"

"Plenty. Zita manages to get food, and I don't ask how. How's my Rosalie doing?"

Anton's uneasiness about the car returned. "Fine. I'll be picking you up for church on Sunday." He hoped she wouldn't notice the patch on the roof, the hole in the ceiling, or question the blanket covering the front seat, something threadbare he'd found in a second-hand shop. When the war was over, he'd take the Rosalie to the best body shop in town for repairs and painting.

"Would you like some tea?"

He just had coffee and kolaches, but he'd drink tea in order to spend a little time with her. "Yes, please. Nothing to eat, though. I just had kolaches with Mr. Dvorak." Leave the food for her and Zita.

Adelka had just gone to the kitchen when he heard a thump. It sounded as if it came from upstairs. He went to the kitchen and stood in the doorway. "Did you hear that noise?"

She took the kettle, which was steaming on the stove, and poured water into the teapot. "I didn't hear anything."

"I did. I wonder if you have an animal upstairs. I'm sure the noise came from up there."

"I think you're imagining things, darling. Go sit down, and we'll have tea."

"I'm going upstairs to check first. Now that you're living down here, if an animal gets in up there it could damage all kinds of things."

"I'll have Zita check later. Have your tea and tell me what you've been doing."

Why was she trying to deter him? "I'll be right back." He took the stairs two at a time. When he got to the top and looked down the hallway, he could see that one of the bedroom doors was closed. He opened the door and saw a young man stretched out on the bed, reading. "Who the hell are you, and what are you doing here?"

The man sat up and swung his legs off the edge of the bed. "I'm a friend of Zita's, and I had nowhere to stay. She's letting me stay here temporarily till I can find a job."

"Does Miss Janakova know about this?" Anton heard a noise behind him.

Adelka was standing in the doorway. "Yes, I know about it."

CHAPTER FIFTEEN

"It's alright, Anton. He's simply a friend of Zita's who needed a place to stay for a short time.

"If that's what's going on, then why didn't you tell me about him when I told you I heard a noise upstairs?"

"Because you had no need to know. Now let's go downstairs and have that tea. Forget you saw him."

There was a lot more to this than they were telling him, and he was sure the man's presence put his aunt in danger. "Let's go to the kitchen."

They sat at the kitchen table, and Adelka poured tea with a smile on her face. He got the impression that she wasn't willing to tell him any more. "I need to know what's going on, and I'm not leaving here until I know the truth." He sipped his tea and leaned back in his chair as if he meant it.

She looked into her cup as if searching for answers there. Then she looked him in the eye. "He's a member of the resistance. The Gestapo is searching for him. I only know that he's waiting for a way to get out of town."

Anton shook his head. "Damn! Excuse my language, but don't you know how dangerous it is, having him here?"

"We're managing."

"What do you mean, you're managing?"

"They came looking for him. They were searching all the houses in Mala Strana. Zita got him into one of my dresses and my gardening shoes, and we pretended he was the cook."

Anton burst out laughing at the ridiculousness of it. "Good God! Next thing I know, you'll be recruited by the resistance. This fooled the Gestapo?"

"Yes." She sipped her tea as if this were an everyday occurrence.

"How long has he been here?"

117

"I'm not certain. I didn't make a note of the date of his arrival. It's been a while."

"Days? Weeks?"

She poured more tea. "I suppose it's weeks."

"You can expect him to disappear from your house very soon. And now I need to use your phone." He signaled his contact for an immediate meeting at Our Lady of Victory Church. "What's his name?"

"All I know is Gustav."

He finished his tea, and as he was walking out the door, said, "Promise me you won't take in any more fugitives."

A smile was her only answer.

#

He waited twenty minutes at the church before the contact appeared. He sat beside Anton when he arrived.

"There's a man named Gustav at my aunt's house. He needs to be removed from there immediately."

"We know. We're working on it."

"You could have let me know."

"Why? You would have been worrying about the situation, a situation you have no control over."

"I am worrying. None of this should have involved my aunt." Then he felt the familiar twinge of guilt for commandeering her car, for involving her to that extent. He was just as guilty as Zita for putting Teta Adelka in danger.

"It certainly wasn't planned. He was on the run and he met a friend who took him there."

"Am I to be the one to get him out of Prague?"

"No. We have other plans. Couple more days, and he'll be gone."

"If he isn't, I'll pick him up myself and drop him off out in the country somewhere like a stray dog."

#

Anton took his tuxedo to the office on Saturday so he could get some work done there before being picked up for the party. He was undecided about whether to give Mrs. Horakova his apartment address. If she insisted on a phone number, he'd give her the one at the office.

Karel was the only one in the office that day. He came into Anton's office and sat in front of the desk. "Looks like you're partying tonight."

"Yes, nothing exciting. A friend of my aunt's gives these little soirees, and she's decided to start inviting me."

"A friend of your aunt's? That doesn't sound like something you'd attend. Unless that woman who was in here the other day would be going too."

Anton's three partners were married, and they tended to be envious of what they considered his carefree bachelor lifestyle. "I'm not sure who'll be there." He shuffled papers on his desk, signaling Karel that he had work to do, but his partner didn't take the hint.

"Vaclav tells me she's a widow."

"Who's a widow?"

"The woman who was here the other day."

Anton smiled in what he hoped was a secretive manner. "Yes, she's a widow. There's a problem with her husband's will."

"Have you made any headway with her?"

"Karel, for God's sake, let's not discuss ladies in that manner."

"I have a feeling she's no lady, but you've probably found that out already, you handsome dog!"

Anton laughed. "Shut up and get out. I have work to do."

Karel got up and went to the door. "The rest of us could live an exotic voyeuristic life through you if you'd only cooperate."

Anton laughed again. "Out!" and Karel went back to his office.

#

He took his tuxedo to the restroom and changed, and then waited by the front door to be picked up. The black Mercedes arrived exactly at eight-thirty. The driver was the same young German who had driven Eliska and him to the previous party and the train station. They arrived shortly before nine, and the maid showed him to the dining room.

Mrs. Horakova captured him at the entrance and took him around for introductions to those he hadn't met before and to

119

several he had met. A hostess couldn't be expected to remember who had met whom, he reasoned, and he greeted everyone with equal cordiality. The hostess introduced him to a young lady named Tanya Horakova, her niece, who had come in from the country for a visit. The butler announced dinner, and Anton found he was seated next to Tanya. He suspected Mrs. Horakova was set on finding a husband for her plain, plump relative. Seated on the other side of her was Frederich Hesse, the young colonel who was to be transferred to Norway within days.

Maria was seated nearby beside Hans Schiller. He needed to tell her about the visit with her father-in-law, but didn't know if he'd have the chance tonight. Maybe when they were dancing—or was this the place to discuss an unpleasant subject? Probably not.

He hadn't eaten all day, and he ate everything he was served and wished for more. He found it interesting that several of the guests left food on their plates. They must be eating better than he was. Tanya chatted with him about her life on the farm and how much she was enjoying Prague. She mentioned that she'd enjoy going to a ballet or the opera, and he figured she was hoping he'd ask to take her. He resisted and hoped Col. Hesse would hear her plea.

The meal ended, and they adjourned to the drawing room. The same trio that played at the last party was in place, already playing a waltz. Maria approached him immediately and asked him to dance. "Did you have a chance to talk to my in-laws?" she asked as they whirled around the floor.

Now that she asked, he guessed an unpleasant subject could be discussed. "I saw your father-in-law. His wife wasn't home. He seemed to be dead set against buying the country estate from you, and since you said you weren't interested in selling to them anyway, I didn't pursue the subject. He's determined to contest the will, and nothing I said changed his mind."

"I knew he'd react like that. So what's the next step?"

"I'd suggest we go ahead and probate the will. I don't see how they can contest it successfully. Your husband had no mental problems, did he?"

"None at all, but that's a miracle, with parents like his."

"Come to the office this week. We'll get the process started."

"Why don't you come to my place? We'll be more comfortable there."

"I'll call you. We'll arrange something."

Hans Schiller had been staring at them as they danced, and he walked up now and cut in. Anton graciously bowed out and went to stand on the side. He wished he hadn't come, and nothing was happening that provided useful information. The evening wore on, and he danced with various ladies without finding out anything for his contact. He had danced with Tanya earlier, and he was looking for her again when he heard a noise outside. It sounded like a muffled gunshot. Then he heard a woman screaming.

Tanya ran into the drawing room from the terrace. "He's been shot," she screamed. Tears ran down her face.

Schiller went to her. "Who is it?"

"Frederich! He's been shot!"

Schiller walked to the terrace and out of sight. When he came back, "Everyone is to stay here till we've had a chance to talk to you. Now I must use the phone." He left the room.

A long night loomed ahead. Now Anton really wished he hadn't come. He remembered when he stood on the terrace with Eliska that it was surrounded by heavy shrubbery, and unless Hesse had accidentally shot himself, someone must have been hiding in the bushes.

Before long the house was filled with Nazi uniforms. They interviewed each of the party-goers, asking for their name, address, and telephone number. An earnest young officer took Anton's information. "You're to report to SS headquarters first thing Monday morning. We'll need a statement."

"Where is SS headquarters?" Best to pretend to be ignorant, as if he had no interest in SS headquarters.

"In the Cernin Palace, on Castle Hill."

"And once I'm in the palace, where do I go from there?"

"Just go up there. Someone will direct you."

121

When they were through, Anton and three others were taken home in the Mercedes. Now they knew where he lived. He had been afraid to lie about it.

CHAPTER SIXTEEN

The sheet she had printed on the mimeograph machine had disappeared from her rag box when Tereza checked it the next morning. The camera and cyanide capsule were still there. Someone in the resistance had a way in and out of the palace without a search, and she was curious, but it was far better that she didn't know. Still, she couldn't help wondering. Was it Olga? She'd never seen the woman arrive or leave, so she didn't know whether she was searched or not. It seemed logical that she would be. Could it possibly be a German who had been turned or who hated what Hitler stood for and had volunteered? This wasn't likely.

She took her cart and went to the supply room. Will was there loading supplies onto his cart for distribution. "Have you thought any more about going out with me some evening?"

She'd been hoping he'd never bring up the subject again, but here it was. If she felt she had to get involved with a German, it should be someone higher up who could give her more information to pass on. "Will, do you know that some women have been killed for being too friendly with Germans. I know you wouldn't want that to happen to me."

"I could go without my uniform. I think I know where to get some civilian clothes."

"Then you'd be in such trouble if they found out. I can't let you do that."

"What if we just meet in the theater and sit together? Then we could leave separately."

"There's another problem. There's the curfew."

"We could go on a Sunday afternoon."

"I'll think about it. I do like you, Will, but a relationship between us could cause such problems."

His face said it all—he had a tremendous crush on her, and he wasn't going to leave it alone. "I'm willing to take a chance . . ."

"Like I said, I'll think about it."

He nodded glumly and continued loading his cart. Tereza noticed a mimeograph stencil lying on the table beside the machine. She started dusting. Would she have time to put it back on the machine and run off a copy after he left? She didn't want to take a chance on asking him where he was going with the supplies. Maybe this was the time for the camera.

He wheeled the supply cart out, and she snatched the camera from her rag box and focused on the stencil. She took several shots, hoping that one would come out well enough to be useful. She put the camera back into the bottom of the rag box. She had just finished mopping the floor when he returned.

"Please think about what I asked you. This war isn't going to last forever, and we could be together with no problems after the war."

Oh, God! Next thing she knew he was going to declare his undying love. She didn't know what to do about him. She began to hope that she would be promoted to something upstairs, as long as it wasn't interpreting the forced confessions of Czech prisoners. "I'll think about it, Will. Really I will." She took her cart and left the room.

She cleaned the offices slowly, hoping to finish at four and go home without being assigned additional duties. Most of the rooms were occupied, and as usual, the occupants cleared out when she came in to clean, but she found no scrap of paper that would be interesting to her bosses.

She was on her way to the cart room when Will approached her in the hallway. "Have you decided about going to the theater with me?"

He was going to drive them both crazy if she didn't agree. "Okay, I'll go this Sunday. Where do you want to meet?"

"Meet me at the Lucerna. There's a movie I think you'd enjoy. I'm glad you decided to go."

124

She hoped this wasn't going to lead to serious complications. She went through the search and flew down the hill on her bicycle. She'd discuss Will with Anton tonight.

#

The theater was so elegant that she was almost glad she came. She stood at the back for a few minutes, admiring the grandeur and letting her eyes adjust to the lower light. She got there early, and the movie hadn't started. She could see that Will hadn't arrived yet. She sat at the end of a row in the center of the theater. He arrived shortly, and she moved over a seat to let him sit on the aisle.

"I'm glad you're here," he said. "This is a funny movie."

They were going to see *The Adventures of Baron Munchausen*, and she wasn't looking forward to it. Will took her hand and held it. Anton hadn't shown up last night, so she hadn't been able to talk to him about the problem of Will. Maybe he'd be there tonight.

The movie dragged on, and she tried to appreciate the humor of it, but these were not humorous times. When it ended, she turned to him. "You leave first. I'll spend some time in the restroom before I go."

"I was hoping we could go to a restaurant and have something to eat before we go home."

"No. That's impossible. You remember what I told you, don't you?"

"No, what did you tell me?"

She got up, squeezed past him, and went to the restroom. She spent several minutes there, combing her hair and fixing her makeup, and when she came out, he was nowhere in sight. She hadn't gone far down the street when she realized that he was following her. She stopped to look in the window of a shoe shop. A pair of wedges with ribbons that tied at the ankle caught her attention. They were summer shoes, on sale now, but she still couldn't afford them. She could see Will's reflection as he stood across the street, watching her.

There was no one she could complain to. The Germans felt it was their right to do whatever they wanted with her, and Olga wouldn't be able to help her. She entered the shop and asked to try on the shoes she'd been admiring. The clerk

125

brought them in her size, and she slowly put them on and walked around while looking in the mirror located on the floor. "I'm sorry, but these aren't exactly what I'm looking for."

"Can I show you something else?"

"No, thanks. Is there a back door I can use?"

The clerk was frowning as if she were concerned about getting involved in something that might turn out to be a problem. "There is no back door. Why can't you leave by the front door?"

"There's a man who's following me. He's still there, across the street."

"You weren't really interested in the shoes. You were just avoiding that young German and wasting my time."

"I'm afraid so. Sorry." She left through the front door. Will was smiling, and he started across the street toward her. She hurried down the street and ended up at the Café Slavia. She went in and sat by a window and ordered tea. Will had followed her all the way, and he came in and sat at a table near her. He was trying to find out where she lived, and she couldn't let him have that information. At first he had been pathetic, then he became irritating, and now he was a little scary.

She drank her tea and got up and went to the restroom. When she came out, he had turned his chair and was looking at her. Just then the waiter came to his table and delivered a plate of food, distracting him. She dashed toward swinging doors that she assumed led to the kitchen. It was the kitchen, and she whispered to the nearest cook, "Which way out?"

The man pointed toward the corner of the room, and she found a door there and ran through it. She was in an alley, and she dashed to the end and came out on a street. She walked quickly to the next corner and turned left. She had lost her bearings, coming out the back door, but this wasn't the time to stop and figure out where she needed to go. She walked from one street to another until finally she recognized a familiar shop. She could get home from there, but she had to make sure he wasn't still following. She stopped in a doorway and looked around. Will was nowhere in sight. Her heart was pounding. She hurried on to her apartment and let herself in.

Tereza sat down at the table and put her head in her hands. She felt like crying, but she wouldn't let herself. This kind of work didn't allow for crying. She hoped Anton would show up soon. She had nothing to eat in the apartment, and she didn't want to go back out to the store. He would bring something, she was sure of it. When he let himself in, he had a jar of what they kept calling goulash in his knapsack, a poor imitation of the real thing.

"I took some photos of a stencil yesterday. I was afraid I didn't have time to put it on the mimeograph machine and run off a copy before Will came back. I hope the photos will be useful."

"You did the right thing. Don't take chances. You're too valuable—especially to me."

She told him about her day with Will, and he nodded. "He's going to be a problem. I don't know what we can do about him, but we can't let him find out where you live. I wouldn't want him to see me coming here, and we definitely don't want him coming here, trying to see you. We haven't used your cover story of your relatives asking me to look after you, and it would be best to save that for emergencies. I think you should refuse to meet him anywhere from now on. Tell him that his following you was disturbing, and you won't agree to any more meetings."

"I agree. He was a little scary today, following me that way. He's obsessed."

"I can see why. I'm obsessed, too. The thought of you being with another man is too much for me to bear."

"I'm obsessed with you, too. I'm in love with you, you know."

"I love you, too." He scooped her from the chair and carried her to the bed. "We don't know how much time we have together." He unbuttoned her dress and kissed her scars, a reminder of her courage. They soon forgot Will and the fact that they might not have tomorrow.

CHAPTER SEVENTEEN

Anton walked up the hill to the Cernin Palace. A Gestapo officer at the door led him into a large waiting room where several people were seated. He recognized most of the party-goers from Saturday night. He decided to sit beside Mrs. Horakova. Tanya, her niece, was beside her.

"Isn't this a terrible situation?" she said. "Now we're all being interrogated like a bunch of common criminals."

"It was terrible that this shooting happened at your house." He couldn't bring himself to say that the shooting was terrible. "I suppose this questioning is routine, however. We all were inside together when it happened except for Tanya, so they can't possibly think one of us is guilty. They're just trying to collect as much information as possible. I'm sure they don't think Tanya did it, either."

A tear rolled down Tanya's cheek. "I wish I'd stayed home. Things like this don't happen in the country."

Mrs. Horakova patted her hand. "We'll see that you get back home as soon as possible."

Maria Dvorakova came through a door at the front of the waiting room. She was smiling as if she'd just returned from a lovely summer picnic. She noticed Anton and stopped by the bench where he was sitting. He stood up when she approached. "How are you? Can I come by your office later today?"

"I'm going to be out of the office most of the day. Are you free tomorrow?"

"I'll come by in the late afternoon. Maybe we can go out somewhere afterward."

Doubtful, Anton thought. "What goes on in the front room?"

"Nothing much. Hans is in there, helping with the questions. It was simple. I was the first one questioned. They called Tanya's name first, but she hadn't arrived yet, so they called me in."

Tanya began to sob. "I suppose I'm next."

"I'll ask if I can go in with you," Mrs. Horakova said.

Maria kissed Anton's cheek. "Till tomorrow."

Hans Schiller came from the interrogation room and called for Tanya.

Mrs. Horakova walked to the front with her. "May I go in with her? She's very upset."

"That won't be possible." He took Tanya's arm and led her through the door.

Anton looked at his watch—it was eight-thirty. "Have you heard any rumors as to who might have shot Frederich?"

"I haven't heard anything," Mrs. Horakova said. "I suppose this is the end of my parties for a while. I can't afford to get in trouble with the SS."

Anton felt a surge of relief that he wasn't going to be invited to any more parties. "Did Frederich have a girlfriend?"

"I never heard of one. He didn't ask to bring anyone to my parties. I was rather hoping that he might like Tanya, and that the two of them . . . well, it might not be the best thing right now, politically, but after the war, who knows what might happen. Of course there were a few other eligible young men there, but now all she can think about is getting back to the country and staying there."

Another cause for relief. He looked at his watch again. Nine o'clock. He'd planned to go to the tailor shop after leaving here and see if the jacket was ready. If it was, he'd take it to the train station and put it in the locker with the suitcase. His contact had called this morning, signaling for a meeting at the Slavia at one, and he had given the one-ring reply that he'd be there. Considering the number of people in the waiting room, he was beginning to wonder.

Tanya came out, and Schiller called Mrs. Horakova. Tanya sat down beside Anton, and Clara Plankova, the woman who had filled him in on all the latest gossip about Eliska at the first party, came over and sat on the other side. Maybe she'd be a better source of information.

"Can you believe this happened?" she whispered. "I feel like giving these people a piece of my mind for calling us all in like this. They can't believe any of us had anything to do with it."

"I can't imagine who did. Have you heard any rumors?"

"I heard he was involved with a maid from one of the hotels, but that's the only thing I've heard about him. That doesn't seem to be a reason for someone to shoot him."

Reason enough, if her family knew she was consorting with a Nazi. "Be careful what you say to them, Mrs. Plankova. You don't want to antagonize the SS, and it might not be a good idea to mention the hotel maid. That might result in much more extensive questioning." They probably knew all about it already.

When Mrs. Horakova came out, they called Mrs. Plankova next. Mrs. Horakova collected Tanya, they told him goodbye, and left. He saw a newspaper on an empty seat, and he couldn't see anyone else he wanted to talk to, so he picked up the paper and started reading.

Witnesses came and went, and the room was almost empty when Anton was called. He followed Schiller into the interrogation room, where his escort sat down at a table with two other men. "I'm Rudolph Schwab," the one in the center seat said, "and this is Rolf Dortmund. I believe you know Col. Schiller."

"Yes, we've met." Anton extended his hand, but no one took it.

"You were at the party at Mrs. Horakova's home this past Saturday evening when Col. Frederich Hesse was shot, were you not?"

"Yes, I was. Several of us were dancing in the drawing room when it happened."

"Can you tell us exactly what happened?"

"I heard a noise—you could call it a pop. It didn't sound exactly like a gunshot. Then Tanya Horakova, Mrs. Horakova's niece, started screaming. She ran into the drawing room from the terrace and said 'He's been shot.'"

"So she was on the terrace when it happened."

"I assume she was, since she ran in through the door from the terrace. I didn't know either of them was outside until she ran into the room."

All three men were taking notes. Schwab was doing all the questioning. "But you said you heard her screaming before she came into the room."

"I didn't know who it was. I just knew someone was outside screaming until she ran in, and then I saw it was Tanya."

"Could you name the people in the drawing room when this happened?"

"Mrs. Plankova was there, dancing with an elderly man whose name I don't remember. The hostess was there, or course. Col. Schiller and Maria Dvorakova were both there, and were dancing together. Those are the only guests whose names I remember. Some of us were invited to dinner, and apparently others were just invited for dancing later. Many had arrived that I'd never met."

"How did you get to the party that night?"

"I was picked up at my office by a young German driver in a Mercedes. Mrs. Horakova said she'd send him for me."

"And how did you get home?"

Anton wanted to glance at his watch, but decided it would be best not to. Let them think he had all the time in the world to answer their questions. However, he was concerned he wouldn't make the meeting with his contact. "The same young man drove me home."

"You were alone in the car with him?"

"No, there were three others. Mrs. Plankova was one of them, and I didn't know the other two."

"You didn't introduce yourselves?"

"We'd just had a rather sobering experience. I guess we weren't in the mood for making polite conversation."

The three of them continued writing for some time. Anton would have liked to read what they were writing, but his German wasn't that good, and it was upside down. His hands were in his lap, and he managed to look at his watch. It was fifteen till one. Would the contact wait if he were late?

"You may go now, Mr. Janak. If you think of any more information pertinent to this case, you are to come back here and ask to speak to the officer in charge."

"Thank you." He got up and left. He spotted Tereza's bicycle through a grove of trees on the way down the hill. He arrived at the restaurant ten minutes late and short of breath. The contact was still sitting at a table, reading a newspaper. Anton sat down across from him.

"Sorry I'm late."

"I understand. I heard what happened. Shall we have some soup?"

"I'm famished." He motioned for the waiter. "What's on the menu today?"

"We have some goulash, and a vegetable puree. There were eggs for omelets, but I'm not sure there are any left."

"I'll take an omelet if you have any. Otherwise, bring the goulash." He hoped it would have at least a little meat in it.

The contact ordered the vegetable puree. "I have no paper for you today. Just an oral assignment. A couple must be picked up at the Church of St. Nicholas in the Mala Strana. Do you know it?"

"Yes, I know it. Just where the Nazis can look down on it from the palace."

"Unfortunately, yes. You must ask for Father Terrelli there. The couple must be taken to a farm near Dobris."

"I know where Dobris is."

"There's a map in the paper. The farm is just beyond the town. If you can pick them up tomorrow morning as early as possible, it would be good to get them out as soon as you can. They have all the necessary papers to get through the roadblocks, which are set up on every road now due to the occurrence on Saturday."

"My passengers won't know the way to the farm?"

"No, they're to be taken in by strangers there. Study the map and burn it before you start out, of course."

"Of course."

The waiter came with the food. The eggs were gone, so Anton ate a meatless goulash and drank coffee. He was sure this couple had something to do with the murder of Frederich

Hesse. Maybe she was the hotel maid he'd been having an affair with, and the man was her husband, or brother, who'd shot Hesse. He wasn't looking forward to driving the Rosalie through roadblocks with its patched roof, but maybe the officers would be concentrating on the people rather than the cars. He just hoped the two he was transporting had adequate documentation for getting past those roadblocks. It had obviously been produced on the spur of the moment, if his thinking about them was correct.

The contact finished his soup. "Any questions?"

"Yes. Has Gustav been removed from my aunt's house?"

"It's happening tonight. But enough about that."

"I'll pick up the couple first thing tomorrow."

"Good luck." The contact left the paper on the table.

Anton took the paper to his apartment and studied the map, and then he burned it in the sink. He left the paper on the table and walked to the tailor's shop, where he found nothing but a smoldering ruin. His Gestapo jacket was gone, either with the Nazis or up in flames. He went to a neighborhood grocery store across the street. "What happened to Mr. Hrabe?" he asked the woman behind the cash register.

She looked as if she were about to burst into tears, but she didn't. "They came and took him away. Then they set the shop on fire."

"Did they search the shop?"

"I don't think so. Did you know him well?"

"No. I had brought some items to him for repair. They're gone now, of course, but that doesn't matter. I feel terrible about his misfortune."

"They're swine. We've been neighbors here for thirty years. His mother was Jewish, he told me years ago. I suppose that's what this is all about."

Anton was angrier now than he'd ever been during the occupation. All he could do to channel the anger was to try to drive two people to safety through Nazi roadblocks, to keep trying to furnish information that would help the cause, and to be ready for whatever he was called upon to do about the Skoda Works. If it meant having an affair with Maria, he would try to do even that. She'd come to the office tomorrow afternoon. At that point, he'd try to put his lovely Tereza out of his mind and concentrate on Maria.

CHAPTER EIGHTEEN

Adelka loved working in her garden, and she had spent the afternoon trimming plants that had stopped blooming until spring came again. She was exhausted by the time she finished; Anton insisted that she not work so hard, but it had to be done, and she enjoyed it in spite of the fatigue.

She often helped Zita prepare meals, but she waited in the library this evening and picked up where she had left off in *Don Quixote* till Zita called her for supper. "Could you bring a tray in here?" she asked when Zita appeared to call her to the dining room.

"Of course. I expect you're tired after all the trimming in the garden. I should have helped you."

"Not at all. You have enough to do with cleaning the house and shopping. Besides, I enjoy working in the garden."

Adelka felt better after eating, and she read until nine o'clock before going to bed. She fell asleep instantly and had been asleep for several hours when she heard noises on the stairs, which reached the downstairs floor near her room. She got up, put on a robe, and opened the door a crack. Gustav was coming down, and Zita was waiting for him at the bottom.

They walked to the door, and Zita went out with him, closing the door quietly behind them. Adelka ran to the window and watched them descend the front steps and go down the sidewalk to the left. They disappeared into the shadows. She looked at the clock—three a.m. She went up the stairs and looked in the room where Gustav had been staying. The bed was unmade. The only other sign that anyone had been there was the ashes in an ashtray that had belonged to her brother Cyril. He had smoked a pipe. Seeing the ashtray and thinking of Cyril made her happy once again that she had helped Gustav.

Zita must have brought a note that had been burned in the ashtray, and now she was out there somewhere in the middle of the night with him. She must be more involved in something clandestine than she was willing to discuss. Adelka admired her courage while fearing for her safety. She said a prayer for both of them before going back to bed and trying to sleep.

#

Zita came home at mid-morning, carrying a bag of vegetables. Adelka was at the small table in the kitchen, having a second cup of coffee. "Zita, I've been worried about you!"

"I'm sorry. Gustav left last night. I needed to go with him. Things got complicated."

"You must tell me what happened."

Zita hesitated, looking as if she wasn't sure she should discuss the events of the night. Finally, "I walked with him because we decided that a couple walking on the street after curfew would be less suspicious than a single man. He was to meet someone at an address near here. No one saw us on the way to the house, but when we got there, the door was locked. No one answered when we knocked. We didn't know what to do, so we sat on the porch and waited."

"You sat there in plain sight with no one home?"

"No, the porch had an enclosed railing, and we sat behind it. After a couple of hours, a car drove to the curb and stopped. We heard a window being rolled down, and someone called his name."

"What kind of car was it?"

"We looked over the railing, but I couldn't tell in the dark. It was an older car, so we decided it was safe. Gustav got in the car with them, and they drove away. I decided I'd better stay on the porch till curfew was over. Then I looked around and didn't see anyone, so I went for groceries."

"I hope he'll be alright. You've no idea where he's gone?"

"No idea at all."

Zita might not be telling the truth about that, but it probably would be best not to know. "Go to bed and get some rest. I'll take care of the groceries." All they could hope for was that Gustav was safe, that he had gone off with someone who would help him. She would ask her friends to pray for him without explaining why their prayers were needed.

CHAPTER NINETEEN

Anton drove the Rosalie to the Church of St. Nicholas and parked on the street. He hadn't been inside the church in years, but his parents had taken him there occasionally when he was young. The opulence of the interior still overwhelmed him. The only people he saw inside were two elderly ladies, one seated near the front to the left of the center aisle and the other on the right. He walked up the aisle and wondered where he could find Father Terrelli. As he neared the altar, he noticed a priest standing in an alcove to the left, looking at him. The man was small and dark—his hair, his eyes, and his skin.

Anton approached him. "Father Terrelli?"

"I'm Father Terrelli."

Say as little as possible. "I'm here to pick up a couple who need a ride."

"Come with me." He led Anton through a labyrinth of anterooms until they came to a closed door. Father Terrelli opened it and revealed two people sitting in a small office. They were dressed simply and appeared to have nothing with them. The man was short and muscular and had a look of mental strain, or maybe it was fear, on his face. The most striking feature about the woman was her short, curly, black hair. Was it dyed? Anton hoped her appearance had been changed enough so that she couldn't be identified as the woman who was having an affair with Frederich Hesse—if that's who she was.

"Where's your car?" Father Terrelli asked.

"It's on the street near the front of the church."

"Please bring it around to the side, and Mr. and Mrs. Martinek will come out a door on that side."

Anton doubted the couple was Mr. and Mrs. Martinek. They looked enough alike to be brother and sister. He went to the car and brought it around to the side of the church, stopping where he saw a door. Father Terrelli came out, followed by the Martineks, and Anton got out of the car. "Sit in the front with me, sir. Mrs. Martinek, please get in the back." If he needed to instruct someone to get the gun from under the dash and start shooting, the man might be the more likely choice. If he were the one who had shot Hesse, his aim was good.

The passengers were silent as they drove through town. "When we get to a checkpoint, try to act, well, if not happy, optimistic," Anton said. "You're going to a farm in the country where you've been promised jobs, and the Germans understand you're hoping to have more food on a farm, so they'd expect you to be happy. Just don't mention the name of the town we're heading for."

"We don't know the name of the town," the man said.

"If they ask you, say the farm is near the town of Rozmital."

"Rozmital. I never heard of it."

"That's okay. Just remember it, both of you."

"We don't speak German, so I don't know how they'll question us."

"They'll undoubtedly have someone that speaks Czech."

They weren't out of town yet, and they could see a checkpoint ahead. The woman started crying. If he turned off now, the guards might have spotted the car and would be suspicious when they came through later. "Please dry your tears," Anton said.

The man reached back and patted her hand. "We're going to be okay, but not if you cry."

She blew her nose and was quiet. Anton pulled in behind the line of cars waiting to be checked. "I don't want to leave Prague," the woman said.

Was that what she was crying about? He'd thought it was because of fear, or because she'd lost her lover to a gunshot. "I don't know why you're leaving, and I don't want to know, but for me to be taking this risk, it must be a matter of life and death." Maybe that would shut her up. Did they even realize he was risking his life by taking them out of the city?

"We appreciate what you're doing," the man said.

The woman said nothing.

They were next in line when the car stalled. Anton wanted to swear, and he would have if not for the woman in the back. He tried to start it with no luck. The car ahead of him moved on, and the guards looked at him. He shrugged his shoulders and tried again. The guards surrounded the car. "Put it in neutral." They pushed him to the side of the street. Still surrounding them, they asked to see their papers. All three produced their documents.

The guard next to Anton asked, "Where are you going—or maybe I should say, where were you going?" The other guards laughed.

The Rosalie was an old car, but previously it had been an object of admiration. Now it was an object of ridicule. Maybe the stalling engine fit in well with the patched roof and holes in the upholstery, in case they noticed. One of the guards who was leaning down to talk to the woman had his hand on the roof. Did he feel the patch? He gave no indication of it.

"We're going to Rozmital. The Martineks have the promise of a job there."

"Why are you driving them?"

"A friend and client of mine asked me to take them. They don't have a car."

"Who is this client?"

"I'm sorry—I'm an attorney, and I can't reveal the name of a client."

"What sort of job is this that's promised to them?"

"They'll be working on a farm just outside Rozmital."

The guards conferred among themselves. The one who seemed to be in charge came to Anton's window. "You can go, if you can get this wreck started." More laughter.

Anton could think of nothing that would give him more pleasure than bashing the man in the mouth, but he smiled and nodded. This undoubtedly was the road to ulcers and other miserable conditions.

"I'll look under the hood," Martinek said. "Maybe I can figure out what's wrong." He and Anton got out of the car, and Martinek immediately started fooling around with wires and other things under the hood. "Now try it."

141

Anton got back in and tried again. This time the engine almost caught, but not quite. The man was doing something else under the hood, and Anton stayed in the car. He was useless when it came to an engine. "Try it again," Martinek said. This time the engine kicked in instantly.

"You obviously know something about cars," Anton said as they drove away. "Thanks for saving us."

"I'm a mechanic. I know how to fix things."

"A useful trait, to be sure." He was beginning to like the man. Surely a place in the resistance could be found for him, and they undoubtedly were heading to a resistance safe house.

They reached another checkpoint at the edge of town, and this time it went smoothly. They showed documents, gave a lengthy explanation, and were on their way. The woman seemed finally to understand the seriousness of the situation, and she gave answers convincingly.

Then they were free of the city and driving through the lovely autumn countryside. A feeling of peace came over Anton. If only he could keep driving, but with Tereza by his side rather than the strangers he was with. They passed through Dobris, and he noticed a café on the main street. He would stop for breakfast on the way back.

Now he was watching for the turnoff to the farm. They passed the small road that came before on the map, and then soon arrived at the road he needed to take. Next he spotted the dirt lane that lead to the farm.

Martinek looked puzzled. "I never saw the town of Rozmital."

"That was only what we were telling the Nazis. The place where you're going to stay is closer to Dobris than anything else."

They arrived at a house that looked as if a prosperous farm family lived there. It was two stories high, looked like it had been freshly painted, and had a front porch with pots of yellow chrysanthemums lining the steps.

A middle-aged woman came out on the porch. She had a broad face and skin weathered a reddish-brown from the sun.

"Stay in the car till I make sure," Anton said. He approached the porch. "I have Mr. and Mrs. Martinek in the car." Again, say as little as possible.

"I'm expecting them. I was told to watch for your car. It's quite distinctive. Bring them inside."

Someone who appreciated the Rosalie. He liked this woman. He motioned for the Martineks to join him, and they followed the woman into the house. Anton would have left, but he wanted a word with her. She showed the pair to separate rooms, and they went in, obviously to have a look at their new quarters. They must be brother and sister, if she gave them separate rooms.

"He's a mechanic," Anton said when she came back to the front of the house. "Our car stalled at a checkpoint, and he managed to get it started again."

"That will be useful. I'm sure we'll find plenty for him to do, both on the farm and otherwise. I wonder if he's handy with explosives."

Anton laughed. "I imagine he'd be a quick learner. As for her, I don't think she's the most stable person in the world."

"Don't worry. She'll be fine here. And if not, we'll take care of her, one way or another."

Anton wondered whether there were other members of the household. Did she have a husband, or children living at home? He decided he shouldn't ask, so he thanked the woman and told her goodbye. The Rosalie started right up again, and he went back to Dobris and found the small café he had seen on the way. An elderly couple was chatting quietly at a table by a front window. He ordered coffee and a roll, whatever they had, and was delighted to find they served the roll with a small pat of butter. It was the first he'd had since the occupation. They must be more relaxed about buying from the black market in the smaller towns. Having all the farms nearby didn't hurt. He took his time and was reluctant to leave, but he had no choice except to return to Prague.

He saw some of the same guards at the checkpoints on the way into Prague, and they remembered him and waved him on after looking at his papers. He put the Rosalie in the garage, and when he walked to the stairs to his apartment, he saw the light was on. He went back and got the gun again and carried it up the stairs. He opened the door and saw Maria Dvorakova sitting at his table, reading the paper he brought home yesterday. She looked up. "Eliska gave me her key to your apartment." She was smiling.

CHAPTER TWENTY

"I'm starving," he said as he put the gun in the box on his bookshelf. Interesting that she had no apparent reaction to the gun. "Are you hungry? I haven't had anything to eat all day." Maybe if he got her out of the apartment he could postpone a confrontation about sex. He didn't want to deal with a woman scorned, especially when she was a friend of Col. Schiller.

"I'm hungry, too. Let's go to my hotel and eat in the café."

"You're staying in a hotel?"

"I live there. The Hotel Paris."

Another independent woman with money. He'd agree to go to the café and nothing more at this time. His earlier resolve to have an affair with her, if that's what it took to obtain information, was fading away.

"After we eat, I'll show you my room. It has a lovely view of the river. Have you ever been there?"

"The café? It's been a while."

"You'll love it again."

Maybe if they tarried long enough, he could use the curfew as an excuse to come home before going to her room. He took a shower and changed clothes in the bathroom with the door locked. Then they went down the stairs. "These stairs need to be repaired," she said. "Aren't you afraid they're going to fall down with you?"

"I'm no carpenter, and the landlady has little money to hire one. I suppose I could try to fix them, but I'm busy most of the time."

They walked to the hotel and entered the café. There were several Germans and a few well-dressed Czechs present. "I think they have smoked salmon this evening," Maria said.

145

They had just finished ordering when the headwaiter approached. "There's a phone call for you at the desk, Mrs. Dvorakova."

She disappeared for a time and then returned. Her face was pale. "I have to leave. Something has come up. I'll come by your office tomorrow." She picked up her purse and left.

Anton chuckled to himself. Saved for the time being. He waited for the food and ate both platefuls. He wished he could take one to Tereza, but it was nearing curfew, and he didn't know how he would have gotten it out of the restaurant even if it hadn't been.

#

He got to the office early the next morning. It was time to get some work done. He'd barely gotten started when Martina informed him that a Mr. Dvorak was there to see him. He thought he'd seen the last of Mr. Dvorak when he went to his house to discuss his son's will, and the older man had refused to budge an inch. Anton went to the front. "Good morning, Mr. Dvorak. Come back to my office. Have a seat, sir. What can I do for you today?"

"I don't know if you've heard the news, but our daughter-in-law's body was found in the river today."

"Maria Dvorakova?"

"Yes, I'm sorry to say. My wife and I have been talking it over, and we made a decision to buy my brother's estate for the price she was asking just to keep it in the family. I called her last night with this news, and ask her to come to our house. When she arrived she seemed very distraught."

"I saw her yesterday afternoon, and she seemed fine."

"I don't know what happened between the time you saw her and her arrival at our house. Anyway, she had her own will with her, and she said she wanted me to keep it. She named me executor, and left everything to my wife and me."

Anton didn't know whether to believe him or not. "And now she's dead."

"Yes. She said she knew my son would have wanted it that way, for us to have everything. She's estranged from her own family. Or was, that is."

146

Had this miserable war turned everyone into savages, and caused the old man and his wife to force Maria to sign the will and then have her killed? The soft-spoken man sitting across the desk from him just didn't fit the part. Maybe Hans Schiller had a problem with her and arranged for her to end up in the river, or murdered her himself. Anton felt guilty about it, but he felt a wave of relief that she wouldn't be trying to seduce him any longer. "I'm really baffled about this. What are the police saying?"

"They're calling it a suicide. They came to us early this morning. They said someone saw her jump, and it took them a few hours to recover the body."

"Who reported seeing her jump?"

"It was a German soldier. Anyway, I brought her will in, and I wonder if you would take care of this for us. My wife and I are eager to get all this behind us. I just hope our previous actions didn't cause the poor girl to take her life."

"It must have been something else," Anton said. "As I said, she seemed fine when I saw her. I'll take care of probating the will for you."

"Would you like a check now?"

"No, when I'm through will be fine. I'll send you a bill. I still have your address in my files from when Maria asked me to contact you."

He showed Mr. Dvorak out and returned to his desk. After reading through the will, he took out the Dvorak file and compared the signature to the one on the slip of paper where Maria had given him information on her in-laws. The signatures appeared to be the same.

\#

He watched the paper for the notice of her funeral. When the day came, he left the office early and walked to the Church of St. Nicholas in Mala Strana, the same church where he had picked up the Martineks. The elderly Dvoraks were there among a small group of mourners. He walked to the front where the closed casket was covered with a spray of white gladiolas.

He stood for a moment with his hat in his hands, pondering the circumstances of her death. When he turned to take a seat

147

he saw, in a far shadowy corner, his contact. That explained a lot. Maria must have been one of them. He pretended not to know or notice the man but took a seat in the middle of the church near the Dvoraks. At least she had a family of sorts there. He wondered if her own family even knew of her death. Mr. Dvorak must have taken care of the funeral and burial.

He'd never know whether she was picked up, tortured, and then tossed in the river, or whether she'd jumped. He imagined that if someone were picked up, they'd be kept for far longer than overnight to extract every bit of information from them. Maybe she jumped because she knew she had been exposed and was about to be taken in for questioning. He walked back to the office haunted by thoughts of how precarious life had become.

CHAPTER TWENTY-ONE

Tereza went to the cart room and checked the rag box. The camera was gone, just as she'd expected, and the cyanide capsule was there. She started cleaning the offices, thinking that if she cleaned the supply room last, Will might be more likely to be out doing other errands. However, she met him in the hallway after doing the second office.

"You ran away from me Sunday. Why did you do that?"

"Because you told me we'd meet in the theater, and then we'd go our separate ways. Then you started following me. You didn't keep your word, so now I know I can't trust you."

He was beginning to look like a petulant child. "I only want to be with you. You're making life miserable for me."

She looked at his cart. It contained only one item, a wooden box. "What's in the box?"

"Don't even ask about it. It's hush-hush." He was smiling again, proud to be part of something important.

She could see that the box had the numbers 7668 stamped on the front. "If it's so hush-hush, why are you wheeling it around in the cart?"

"It has to go for repairs."

"You're going to repair it?" She knew he wasn't, but hoped for more information.

It wasn't forthcoming. "No, but enough about the machine. When are you going to the movie with me again? Sunday afternoons are nice, and then afterwards I could meet you at your apartment if you don't want to walk with me there."

"I don't trust you, Will. You told me one thing about last Sunday and did something else. I'm not going with you, period!"

He was pouting again. "I could make life very difficult for you here, you know."

"And I could make life difficult for you, too," she said, hoping he'd think she was implying that she had a connection with a higher-up who would deal with him. She turned and walked away, hoping she'd called his bluff and that he wouldn't be accusing her of stealing or spying. She felt sure he wouldn't accuse her until he was positive she wouldn't go out with him any more. And maybe if he thought she was involved with an officer, he wouldn't harass her any more.

She wondered what the machine was that she saw on his cart. It must be something plenty special, if Will called it hush-hush. She doubted she'd ever be able to get her hands on it, but she'd let Anton know she'd seen it. Maybe he'd know what it was, and maybe he should report its presence at the palace.

She went outside at noon to shake out her duster and sit on a bench and eat the bread and cheese she'd brought for lunch. If ever she had to make a quick escape, she might be able to scale the wall surrounding the patio. The wall was six feet high and made of solid brick, but in one corner, a few bricks were chipped. Possibly there was a chance for a foothold. If she made it to the top, she could drop to the ground among the trees on the other side. She hoped that day would never come.

She finished her food and wished she could spend the afternoon outside. Since it wasn't possible, she started to go inside when Will came through the door. "I'm sorry about our argument earlier. I hope you'll forgive me. I love you, you know."

"Will, please. The situation is hopeless between us."

"I see soldiers on the streets with Czech girls when I go out in the evenings. What's so wrong about it?"

"Do you know what's going to happen to those girls when the war's over?"

"We're going to win. Nothing will happen to them. They'll be part of the ruling class here, and you would too if you'd only listen to reason."

So he thought the Germans were going to win. Of course he did—he was one of them. She wished for an easy solution, but she knew there wasn't going to be one. Maybe she should go to bed with him on Sundays after a movie, and that would keep him quiet. Her revulsion at the thought let her know that wasn't going to work. She felt immense gratitude that at that moment Olga came through the door.

"Where have you been, Tereza? I've been looking all over for you. Colonel Schwann wants to see you upstairs."

"I'm sorry. I was just shaking my duster and having lunch. I'll go up right away."

The look on Will's face could best be described as stricken. Tereza found herself feeling sorry for him again. She knew what was going through his mind. She put the duster back on her cart and went upstairs to Schwann's office. She waited for the woman typing at a desk in the outer office to notice her. The woman looked at her through thick glasses. Her hair was drawn back in a tight knot. "Yes?"

"I was asked to report to Colonel Schwann."

"Have a seat."

Tereza sat on one of a row of chairs at the side of the room. Would she be asked to work in this room? It was bright and airy, with windows on two sides. A table sat by the windows. Maybe she'd be asked to sit there and interpret documents. At least she'd be able to look outside. The woman disappeared for a few minutes, and then she returned and went back to her typing. A half hour passed, and Tereza sat there, doing nothing. Then Schwann appeared. "I'm sorry to keep you waiting. I was on a long distance phone call. Come in."

She went into his office. "Have a seat. Would you like coffee?"

"Yes, please." Some real coffee would be a treat. Maybe there would be food, too.

He buzzed the lady in the outer office, whom Tereza assumed was his secretary. "Bring us coffee, Miss Bauer, and some of those pastries left over from the meeting."

He was looking at her now, all smiling charm. "I've put in a request to have you transferred to my office. We have an abundance of translation that needs to be done and a shortage of personnel to do it. You'd fit in perfectly here. Your talents are wasted on the cleaning staff."

"What sort of translation would it involve?"

"The Allies are constantly putting out propaganda to stir up the people. They drop it from the sky, mostly. We need it translated into German in the most correct way in order to know how to refute this misinformation. You may have noticed a stack of papers on the table in the outer room. That's the amount that's accumulated since we last had someone who could do the job for us." Miss Bauer interrupted with a tray loaded with a coffee service and a plateful of pastry.

"Would you pour the coffee, my dear?" he said.

"Certainly." Tereza poured for both of them. "Would you care for sugar or cream?"

"No thanks. I take mine black. Help yourself to a pastry. I've had some already in the meeting."

Tereza enjoyed the fragrance of the coffee just as much as the taste. She ate one pastry and helped herself to another. Schwann was smiling, as if he understood how much she was enjoying the food. "I'll get Miss Bauer to bring a bag, and I want you to take the rest of these home with you."

Anton would be thrilled. At least six of the large pastries remained on the plate. They'd have enough for supper and breakfast, too. She finished the second pastry and sipped her coffee. "When will I be transferred to your office?"

"On Monday. The paperwork will be complete by then. Until then, you'll need to continue with your cleaning job."

She thought that she probably wouldn't have much chance to collect intelligence in this office unless she could overhear Schwann's telephone conversations. She noticed his door was closed while he talked as she waited in the outer office. Her camera and cyanide capsule would have to be removed from the cleaning cart, and it would be impossible for her to have the camera here in Schwann's office. Maybe she could conceal the capsule in her bra.

Another drawback to the change was that Miss Bauer didn't like her; she'd sensed that from the moment she walked in. Miss Bauer probably didn't like anybody, but Tereza didn't want any enemies among the Nazis, not even a secretary. On the other hand, she'd be away from Will unless he delivered supplies here.

"I'll report for my cleaning job as usual for the rest of the week." She couldn't help noticing he had a couch in his office. It appeared to be of an olive green velvet fabric with lush velvet pillows in red and beige stacked on the ends. She finished her coffee as Miss Bauer came in and bagged up the pastries without a word.

She took the bag and went back to her cleaning cart. Would she be able to take the food out when they searched her? She hadn't thought of that when Schwann offered it; she'd only thought of how nice it would be to have it. If the search officer wouldn't let her take it out, she'd have to leave it.

She saw Will only once as she finished the cleaning. He walked past her with his head down and didn't say anything. She hoped he wouldn't be trouble. When she got to the search line, Natalie was there. "I hear you're going to be working upstairs." She didn't appear happy about it.

Tereza laughed. "How did you hear that so fast? I just found out myself."

"I have my sources. I didn't know you spoke German."

"I grew up in the Sudetenland. My mother was of German descent."

"How did you end up in Prague?"

"I was hoping for a job as translator, and now it looks like that's going to happen." Just stick to the cover story.

"Good luck up there."

Tereza couldn't help feeling there was some envy behind her words, or was it concern that one of their own would soon be involved with a Nazi officer. "Thank you. I appreciate your good wishes."

"What's in the bag?"

"Some pastries they gave me in the office upstairs. They were left over from a meeting. Would you like one?"

Natalie looked as if she knew "they" didn't give Tereza the pastries, the colonel did. "Yes, I'll take one and eat it right now, because I don't think you'll be able to leave with those."

"We'll see." She opened the bag and Natalie took one. "I'll get ahead of you in line so you can have time to eat that before you go in."

Natalie brightened a little. "Thank you."

153

Tereza went into the search office, and the first thing the officer asked was, "What's in the bag?"

"Pastries that Colonel Schwann gave me. He said I could take them home."

"Okay, put them down over there for now." She searched Tereza thoroughly, and then picked up the bag and dug through the pastries to make sure nothing suspicious was hidden there. She handed the bag to Tereza.

The search officer's hands had touched everyone who had been cleaning all day, and they couldn't have been very clean, but Tereza didn't care. Food was too scarce to worry about such things. She wouldn't tell Anton; she didn't want to take away from the surprise.

She put the linen tablecloth on the table when she got home. She had bought needles and thread at the grocery store where she shopped, and she had mended a tear where the lace edge had separated from the linen. She put the pastries on a plate and set it in the middle of the table. She wished for a candle, but she hadn't seen any since arriving in Czechoslovakia.

Anton arrived shortly with a dish of potatoes that had a small bit of something in them that looked like ham. He saw the pastries on the plate. "Where did you get those?"

"I have news. Actually, I have two bits of news. Let me start with this. Will had something on a cart in a wooden box. He said it was hush-hush, and he was taking it for repairs. I couldn't get him to tell me what it was."

"How big was it?"

She extended her arms. "About this long, this wide, and this high."

"Were there any markings on it?"

"The numbers 7668 were stamped on the front. That was all. I don't know if it's important, but I thought you should know."

"Definitely. What's your other bit of news?"

"I was called upstairs today by an officer, Colonel Schwann. He said I'm to be transferred to his office starting Monday. I'll be translating propaganda documents from Czech into German. It will get me away from Will, but I don't think

I'll have much chance to collect information. Unless I can overhear the officer's phone conversations, but that doesn't seem likely. He kept me waiting for a half hour while he was on the phone, and his door was closed the entire time."

"And the pastries?"

"They gave me coffee and pastries while I was there. Then they told me to take the rest of them home."

Anton's face was grim. "I don't like this."

She knew what he meant. "I don't like it, either, but I have no choice. However, the man has a wife and children. I saw their photo on his desk. She's a beautiful woman with two little blonde kids."

"And they're in Germany and he's here."

"Please don't worry. I can handle this without going to bed with him. He's very courteous—it's not like he's going to force me to have sex with him. I'll tell him I'm engaged to a man back in the Sudetenland."

"Don't do that. He'll insist on a name and address so he can have the man drafted and sent to the front."

"Okay, I won't. But you're not to worry. It's just not going to happen."

He took her in his arms. "I just want to look after you and see that nothing bad happens to you."

She kissed him. "How about looking after me in bed right now?"

He smiled for the first time since their conversation began.

CHAPTER TWENTY-TWO

Anton met the contact at Our Lady of Victory Church to give him the coded message about the wooden box Tereza had seen. "Have you heard any more about the operation we discussed before?"

"Erik and Jakub will be gone for a while, and when they return to Prague, we'll have an answer for you. This has to do with two railroad bridges. I can't say any more now. I'll give you the details as soon as I can." The contact handed him a message in a newspaper, and Anton took it to his apartment to decode. It said, "Take Erik and Jakub to U Mansfelda Restaurant in Pilsen eleven hundred Friday. Erik and Jakub will go with contact. Code: The food is good here."

Damn, he was going to have to drive the teenagers back to Pilsen. He wondered whether he'd ever see them again, after what happened last time. He also wondered why they couldn't take the bus, or the train. If they could be trusted to take part in something that had to do with the Skoda Munitions Works, they surely could be trusted to get themselves to Pilsen.

He'd have to let them know, and he went first to the Kolkovna Restaurant where Jakub worked. Jakub wasn't there. He asked a waiter he didn't recognize and was told it was Jakub's day off. "Do you have his address?"

The waiter went to the back and came back with a slip of paper. A street in Old Town. Anton found the address after some looking and knocked on the door. A woman answered, holding a baby on her hip. "Is Jakub here?"

"Jakub!" she yelled.

He came to the door looking as if he just woke up. When he saw it was Anton, he came outside and closed the door. "What's up?"

"I need to take you back to Pilsen Friday. Can you get time off at the restaurant?"

"They understand. I can get off. I'll meet you where we met last time."

"Who's the girl with the baby?"

"My sister. Her husband works in Brno."

"The two of you live here?"

"My parents, too."

Anton wondered whether Jakub supported the whole family. "Do you have a way to let Erik know?"

"No, I don't have a car. None of us does. As you know, he doesn't have a phone."

"I'll have to drive back out there again. I'll see you Friday at eight. Better pack a few things to take with you."

He'd go on out to the farm right now and let Erik know. He didn't like going to his house—Erik's parents looked at Anton with both suspicion and fear. Apparently the fear was strong enough that they didn't give him any arguments when he asked to speak to Erik.

It was a nice day for a drive in the country. One of the last nice days of the fall, he suspected. And there were no roadblocks, which was a bonus. He hadn't begun to do anything about Maria's will, but the Dvoraks had enough money that what they'd get from her could wait a bit. He'd start the process tomorrow.

He arrived at the farm and knocked on the door. Erik's father answered. He didn't say anything, just stood there looking at Anton as if he were the SS. "Is Erik here?"

"He's at the barn, shoeing the horse. Can I help you?"

"I need to talk to him. It's about a job in Pilsen."

The man nodded and pointed to the barn. Anton found Erik there trimming a brown mare's right front hoof. "You're wanted in Pilsen again," Anton said.

"What this time?"

"They don't tell me things like that. I'm to take you there Friday."

Erik didn't look pleased. "I hope this isn't another waste of time."

158

"I hope not, too. I'll pick you up at eight-thirty. You'll need to bring some things with you."

He drove back to town slowly and reluctantly went to his office when he arrived in Prague at noon. He tackled the stack on his desk, trying to forget he had to go to Pilsen Friday.

#

Jakub was waiting on the corner. He tossed his knapsack into the backseat and climbed in beside Anton. "I wish I knew what this is all about."

"I suppose you'll learn eventually."

"Do you have a feeling it has something to do with the Skoda Munitions Works?"

"I have no idea. All I know is, I'm supposed to drive you there."

They arrived at Erik's house and he was ready with a small suitcase. His parents were nowhere in sight. "Ready for a big operation?" Jakub asked.

"I guess so." He didn't sound enthusiastic.

They found the U Mansfelda Restaurant after getting lost for a few minutes. It was five after eleven. They went in and took a table in the middle of the restaurant. The waiter came, and they ordered what he described as chicken and dumplings. They'd been waiting for their order for ten minutes when a man walked in the door.

Anton thought he looked familiar, and as he got closer, he realized it was Martinek, the man he'd taken to the farm along with his wife. He came to the table and shook hands with all of them as if they were old friends. "The food is good here," he said.

So he'd been recruited already. Anton had had a feeling he'd be an asset to the resistance. After all, he was probably the man who shot Frederich Hesse. "Mr. Martinek. How are you?"

"Call me Alek. I'm very well. How are you?"

"I'm well also. We've ordered already. We're hungry after the long drive."

"I've eaten already. I'll just have some coffee."

"How's your wife doing?"

159

"She's doing well. She decided she likes life in the country after all. She's fitting right in, helping in the fields. She's even learned how to milk the cows."

Several Germans were eating in the restaurant, and Anton couldn't think of anything to talk about that wouldn't arouse suspicion. He was immensely curious to know what had happened when the Gestapo realized one of their members was missing, but it was impossible to ask Alek, and he probably wouldn't know anyway. If ever the body were found, there would be reprisals. He hoped they had hidden it well enough that that would never happen. He hoped they'd think the man had deserted.

Their food arrived and as Anton had imagined, it was mostly dumplings in a little broth. They found no chicken. Anton couldn't help wondering if the Germans sitting nearby got the chicken with their dumplings. Just one more reason to work against them.

When they finished, he paid the bill. Outside, he took the rosary Jakub had given him from his pocket and handed it to him without saying anything. They separated after shaking hands—Alek and the boys walked on down the street, and Anton went to his car.

CHAPTER TWENTY-THREE

Friday, and Tereza's next-to-last day cleaning on the lower floor. She wouldn't miss the work, and she wouldn't miss Will. If she could avoid him today and tomorrow, all would be well. She started with the offices again. Her camera and cyanide capsule were still in her rag box, and she assumed they'd be gone by tomorrow. Her cart might be turned over to someone else by Saturday afternoon. She found nothing to photograph as she went from office to office, and she wondered if the expense of her training and flying her to Prague was worthwhile.

She had finished half the offices when she went outside on the patio to shake out her duster and have lunch. She'd had one of the leftover pastries for breakfast; the last one would be lunch. She was sitting on a bench, licking her fingers, when Schwann came onto the patio. "Having lunch?"

"Yes. I just finished."

"I came down to ask you to come and have lunch with me."

Her stomach began rebelling against the pastry she had just put into it. This was going to get complicated. "That's very nice of you, but I've had enough already."

"How about some coffee then, and a dessert? Our chef makes a very nice mousse."

"I'm afraid I won't have time to get my cleaning done if I come upstairs."

He smiled as if he were amused by her naiveté. "Don't worry about it. I'll see that it gets done."

Was he expecting her to spend the afternoon with him? What could she say to deflect his attentions? "I just wouldn't want to get in trouble."

He laughed. "You won't get in trouble. I'll see to it. Put your cart away and come upstairs."

Damn, he couldn't wait till she started working upstairs. "Yes, sir."

"And don't call me sir. When we're alone together you can call me Lukas. Of course, when we're in the company of others, such as Miss Bauer, you'll have to call me Colonel Schwann."

She took the cart and put it away. Then she went to the bathroom and washed her face. She had no makeup on, and she wanted to keep it that way. Her dress was faded and a little too large, another plus for deterring the interest of Schwann and Will. Then she thought about the scars on her stomach and leg. Having sex with Schwann would expose the scars. Would he begin to wonder whether she was the one who landed in that tree? This was another good reason to avoid his advances.

She climbed the stairs slowly to the next floor and went into Schwann's reception area. Miss Bauer looked at her with more venom than Tereza ever experienced before. Was she in love with her boss? It was entirely possible—he was handsome, suave, and friendly. Working in the same room with her would be a challenge.

"Colonel Schwann asked me to come up to his office."

"I know. Go on in."

Schwann was just finishing lunch. He stood up and motioned for her to sit across the desk. He buzzed Miss Bauer. "Bring coffee and dessert, please." He turned to Tereza. "You see how easy that was. I think you and I are going to get along well. You're sure you don't want any more lunch before dessert?"

"I'm sure. I'm not sure I can hold dessert."

"Just a few bites, at least. You know, you have a very slight accent that I find charming. I'm sure it's the result of growing up speaking both languages."

She hoped he wasn't going to start asking about her background. Some of that information had been knocked out of her head when she landed in that tree—it now seemed that had happened years ago, but her mind still wasn't clear at times. "I'm fortunate to be able to speak both languages. It's given me the opportunity to work as a translator, which I've always wanted to do."

Miss Bauer came with a loaded tray and set it on the desk. "You can take the rest of the afternoon off," Schwann said. "Go shopping and have a wonderful afternoon."

Miss Bauer didn't look pleased, but she managed to mumble, "Thank you, sir."

"Please close the door as you leave."

This was going to be difficult. Tereza poured coffee for both of them. Two lovely slices of torte sat on plates on the tray also. She wished she had more of an appetite for something so special.

"Please, try the torte with your coffee."

She took a few bites. "It's delicious."

"You and I will have a long relationship. Your parents are gone—I read your file, of course. You need someone to look after you."

Was he planning to set her up in a luxury apartment as his mistress? Things were moving too fast. She smiled. "I've done a pretty good job of looking after myself so far."

"You certainly have, and I admire you for it."

She looked at the photo of his wife and children—at least she assumed it was his wife and children.

"Yes, I'm married. I'm also very lonely here. I'll be frank with you. You've captured my heart in a way that no other woman has in years. That day you came upstairs to help arrange that table for our meeting, well, I felt as if I had met someone very special. I want to spend time with you. I think you'd be happy in Berlin, after the war."

Good God, just like Will, he was planning out her entire life. "Sir, you're making my head spin. I don't know what to think of all this."

"Lukas! Call me Lukas!" He got up and took her hand. "Come to the couch with me."

He sat beside her and kissed her. It was a nice kiss, as kisses go, but he just wasn't Anton. He put his hand on her knee. "I can do so much for you."

She could think of only one way to discourage him. "Sir, Lukas, there's something I must tell you. This is awkward.

163

This isn't the right time of the month . . . if you know what I mean."

A look of disappointment came over his face, but only for an instant. "I understand, my dear. That's no problem. It's your company I want. Please sit here with me. I want to hear all about your childhood. I want to know everything about you."

Oh, God. Could she remember the names of the schools she was supposed to have attended? Was this a test? "First, I want to hear all about you. Where were you born?"

"I was born in Hamburg. My father is involved in shipping."

The phone rang in the outer office. "I'll have to answer that." He left the room and closed the door behind him. She couldn't hear what he was saying, but he came back in looking glum. "Unfortunately, we'll have to postpone our talk. I'm being summoned to a meeting that will last the rest of the day. I'm going to come in tomorrow, and we can make plans for the weekend."

She nodded and smiled. "I'll see you tomorrow." There would be no deterring this man; she could see that. And he was going to want to take up so much of her time that Anton would know what was going on. She didn't know what to do except to talk it over with Anton.

She went back downstairs, where she saw Natalie in the hallway. "I've cleaned the rest of the offices. I didn't get to the supply room yet." Her tone wasn't friendly.

"Thanks. I'll take care of the supply room." She got her cart.

As she headed for the supply room, Will was coming down the hallway with a cart stacked high with forms of some kind. "Where have you been?"

She wanted to tell him it was none of his business, but then he was a German, after all, and she was hesitant to provoke him. "I had to go upstairs. They wanted to show me what my duties will be when I go to work up there next week."

"I'm sorry for the way things have gone with us lately. I hope we can continue our relationship after you've gone to work upstairs."

164

"Please let me think about all this, Will. I'm concentrating so hard on figuring out what I need to do upstairs that my head is spinning. I'm going to clean the supply room now."

When she got there, she saw a mimeograph stencil drying on the table. The hallway was deserted. She took out the camera and started taking one shot after another. Then Will was standing beside her. "I forgot . . . what are you doing?" The last was shouted.

He grabbed her left arm with his right hand. She smashed his larynx with the side of her hand just as she'd been taught at Catoctin. His face first showed surprise, then outrage. He dropped her arm, clutched his throat, and sank to his knees. His gasping and struggling to breathe was horrible. She stepped back as he fell forward. If he wasn't dead, she'd have to finish him off somehow.

Was there room for his body in the metal cabinet, and did he have a key? She put her hand in his pants pocket, and he clutched at her wrist. Then his grip slowly loosened and his hand dropped to the floor. She found a key ring in his left pants pocket. Surely there was a key to the cabinet on it. She felt for a pulse, and there was none.

The fourth key she tried opened the lock, and she could see that there was just room under the bottom shelf to stuff his body. She dragged him to the cabinet and pushed him in. She was shaking, but she knew this was no time to panic. She took a copy of each paper from the cabinet, folded it, and put it in her pocket. Now the doors were locked again, and Will's keys were in her pocket. Where was the camera? She had dropped it when Will grabbed her arm, and she found it on the floor. That went into her pocket, too, along with the cyanide capsule.

She wheeled the cart back to the cart room, parked it, and went outside. If someone saw her climbing over the brick wall, it was all over. She considered throwing the items in her pockets over the wall and trying to retrieve them later. However, she couldn't leave by the front door; it was too early for the search, and she was sure that door was locked until time for the employees to leave.

She went to the corner of the wall and put her foot against a chipped spot. She could barely reach the top of the wall with her fingertips. She raised herself slowly until she could get her hands on top of the wall. Someone was walking along outside the patio; she could hear leaves crunching. Did they patrol the outer perimeter of the palace? She waited till the sound went away.

She managed next to get her arms on top of the wall, and then to swing a foot up to the top. Gradually she raised her body till she was lying on a foot-wide layer of bricks on the top. Then she dropped to the other side. She was in a wooded area, and she started downhill; it was the only logical way to go. She came alongside the main road to the castle, and she stayed in the woods until they gave out. Then she was on the road. She wished for her bicycle, for flying down the rest of the way. She loved that bicycle and would miss it.

She was coming to intersecting streets now, and she saw the Church of St. Nicholas off to the right. She headed for it, keeping the spires in view all the time. She had stopped in the church once on her way home and found it stunning compared to her family's modest church in Schulenburg. She'd go in there and call Anton. They must have a phone somewhere.

The church towered over her now. She opened the front door and went inside. The church was empty except for a priest, who was doing something at the front, and Tereza headed for him. Her legs had been shaking all the way down the hill, and now they were failing to hold her. She reached the front pew and sat down.

The priest turned toward her. He was a small, dark man, not at all like their priest at home, either. He came over to her. "Are you all right, Miss?"

She started crying. "A confession, father. I just killed a man."

He didn't look all that surprised, but then this was Prague, and not Schulenburg. "Tell me what happened."

"At the palace—I killed a man," she said between sobs.

"Don't say anything more now. Let's go to my office." He helped her up and took her through some anterooms—she wasn't sure how many—till they reached an office. She didn't make it to the chair in front of the desk; she collapsed on a couch near the door. He sat down beside her. "I'm Father Terrelli. Do you want to tell me what happened?"

"This is a confession, father. Have you ever heard of the Office of Strategic Services?"

"Of course."

"I'm an OSS agent. I was taking photos in the supply room of the palace when I was seen by the supply clerk. I killed him. I'm afraid I'm in serious trouble."

"My, my." He seemed to be amazed not that she had killed someone, but that such a pretty little thing could kill someone. "You'll be fine here. Would you like a cup of tea?"

She laughed, half-hysterically. "Yes, I'd love it."

He disappeared for a while and came back with two cups of tea. She had managed to compose herself during his absence. She sipped the tea with gratitude. "I need to use the phone."

"It's not safe. Or it might be safe, but I'm not sure. Nothing is sure these days. We can get word out to someone if you wish."

She didn't want to reveal Anton's name to anyone at this point, and she didn't know his address. All she had memorized were his phone numbers. His law office would be easy enough to find by someone wanting to get a message to him, but she was reluctant to talk about him. "I'll have to think about what I need to do. This church is so close to the palace, I think this will be one of the first places they'll look for me when they find the body."

"Where is the body?"

"I put it in a metal cabinet and locked the doors. I have the keys. I hope they won't find it till tomorrow."

"You'll be safe here till tomorrow. You'd probably be safe here indefinitely. I think we'll turn you into a nun for the time being."

He went to a cabinet in the corner and produced a complete nun's wardrobe. "Go ahead and put these on over your clothes."

She did, and he helped her adjust the headgear. "Now, some glasses." He took some small, gold-rimmed glasses from the cabinet. They were clear glass and didn't distort her vision

167

at all. "If they come in, you'll go to the altar and pray. I think that's safest. This is an amazing transformation."

"What about my shoes?"

"Shoes are hard to come by these days, so I think those are fine. They look like something a down-and-out nun might wear."

She couldn't help laughing. He was making her feel better all the time. It seemed he was accustomed to helping those in trouble with the Nazis. "Father, do you do this sort of thing often?"

"No more often than I have to. It's hard on my nerves."

"Believe me, I understand."

"How about helping me with the programs for the Sunday mass? I had just run them off on the mimeograph before you came in."

"I'd be delighted to have something to do." She went with him into an adjoining room where the programs were stacked on a table, and they began folding.

#

She woke up on the hard little cot where she'd gone to sleep the moment her head was on the pillow. She thought she'd be awake all night, listening for boots breaking down doors, but that hadn't been the case. She'd slept through the night and was now wondering what time it was. She was wearing her dress; the nun's habit was draped over the only chair in the room. It stood in front of a small writing table. A two-drawer chest completed the furniture.

She had taken everything from her pocket and placed it in the drawer of the writing table. She took the things out now, including her watch. It was seven o'clock. She put everything back into her pocket and put on the nun's habit, managing the headgear on her own, and wandered around till she found Father Terrelli's office. "I've just requested breakfast for two. Come in and have a seat."

A lady arrived soon, the same one who had brought them soup last night. She put down a large tray with a coffee pot, two cups, and two plates. On the plates were eggs, the first she'd seen since she came to Prague. "Eggs!" she said. "I'm amazed. What a treat."

"Now and then we have folks from the country who bring us things. It doesn't happen often. You just happened to be here at a serendipitous time."

Tereza was almost through with her food when the priest's phone rang. He picked it up and listened for a moment. "Go to the altar," he said.

She knelt in front of the altar and folded her hands in prayer. Her eyes were closed. She heard them come in; it sounded like several footfalls behind her. It didn't take them long to find the body and figure out what happened. Someone said "We need to search the church, Father. We're looking for a fugitive. She's dangerous. She's already killed one man, and she won't hesitate to kill again."

"Please let me show you around."

She would have sworn the voice she heard talking to Father Terrelli belonged to Schwann. She couldn't look, and she knew they wouldn't go behind the altar so she could see them. That was forbidden, and surely even the Nazis knew it. They had a Catholic background, too; at least she assumed they did since the German side of her family was Catholic as well as the Czech. She could hear them exiting to the left, through the anterooms leading to Father's office. She hoped he'd managed to hide her plate. It sounded as if there were at least five of them.

Someone touched her shoulder. "Anton! Thank God."

"Come with me. Quickly."

They rushed to the front of the church and went outside. A cab was waiting, and he helped her into it and got in beside her. She was afraid to say anything. Just ride, with his hand holding hers. That was all she needed for now.

They stopped on a side street, and she could see a stairway going up to what looked like an upstairs apartment. They got out, and Anton paid the driver. She followed him up the stairs and into the apartment. "How did you find me?"

"The network. It does work, most of the time." He took her in his arms. "You make a mighty sexy nun."

She took off the headgear. "Do you know what happened?"

"Tell me all about it. But first, take off that garment."

She pulled the habit off over her head and told him everything, beginning with the meeting with Schwann. When she was through, she unloaded the items from her pocket and put them on his table. She held up the key ring. "One of these keys is for the metal cabinet where I put the body. I don't know what the others are for. This stack of papers contains a sample of everything that was in the locked cabinet. The camera contains some photos of the stencil I was taking pictures of when Will came in.

"I'll get all this to my contact as soon as I can. He'll know what to do with it. What are the papers that were in the cabinet?"

"I looked over them last night in my little cell at the church. They seemed to be standard forms for one thing and another. Maybe someone else can make more of them than I did. Father Terrelli is a wonderful man. I'm so glad he was there when I came staggering into that church."

"He's proving to be most helpful to our cause."

"You've had some contact with him before?"

"Yes, but enough about that. How do you like my apartment?

"It's very nice. Much nicer than mine. What are you going to do with me?"

"You mean eventually? We'll talk about that. Right now we're going to bed so I can hold you close."

CHAPTER TWENTY-FOUR

The phone rang twice, stopped, and then rang twice again. Anton would meet his contact at the house on Skolska Street at two o'clock. He'd never been to that meeting place before, and he wondered whether this had something to do with the plan for the Skoda Munitions Works.

He looked at Tereza as she slept next to him. He was sure she realized it already, but they'd have to discuss the fact that what had happened would make an extraction necessary. He hated the word. It sounded like a bad experience at a dentist's office. He hated it even more because it meant she would have to leave him.

He got up, dressed quietly, and went down to the bakery. "I'm hungry this morning," he told Mrs. Svobodova. "What do you have for a hungry man?"

"No wonder you're hungry. It's almost noon." I have some yeast rolls and a tiny bit of jelly left in a jar. There's no butter, of course."

"Just give me what you have." He went back upstairs with four big rolls and the jelly.

Tereza was sitting up in bed. "Let's get married. It's the next logical step, since I love you and you love me."

He put the food on a plate and set it on the table. "That's an excellent idea." He wondered why he hadn't thought of it himself.

"I've been thinking about it for a while, and now I know it's the thing to do. You realize I'm going to have to go back to the states, if I can get there. Then I'll be reassigned somewhere else. I'd like to be married to you while that's going on. I'll be back here immediately when the war's over."

"You're wonderful. But I have no idea what's involved with getting married. I'm reluctant to let you leave the apartment, too."

"Please go to City Hall and find out what we need to do. I'll leave the apartment only once, for the ceremony. We'll be married in the Church of St. Nicholas when I come back after the war. Father Terrelli will perform the ceremony."

Based on what he knew of Father Terrelli, he couldn't help wondering whether he'd survive the war. There was no need to mention this to Tereza, however. He sat at the table and coded a message: Extraction needed. Please advise. He was feeling better about it somehow, now that she had suggested marriage. He'd give the message to the contact when he met him at two. "I have to go out this afternoon. I'll go to City Hall and find out what we need to do to get married. You can't get married in the name Tereza Valentova. Alexandra Novakova would be better. I'd feel as if the marriage were truly legal if we use your real name. Of course you'll always be Tereza to me."

"Maybe you could use Tereza as my middle name. Alexandra Tereza Novakova."

"Come and have some rolls. We even have a little jelly."

"I wish I had my linen tablecloth. That's lost forever, like my bicycle. I had gotten attached to those things, too."

"They may be watching your apartment and questioning the landlord, if they learn that the address you gave them was a fake and they find out the truth. We don't dare go there. It probably isn't wise to try to recover the bicycle, either. I'm sorry about those things."

"There's nothing to be done about them now." She looked at the food. "You eat three rolls, and I'll have one. I had breakfast just before the Nazis showed up at the church. I even had an egg."

"I'll just have two. Save the other one for when you get hungry while I'm out."

"What about your landlady? Doesn't she bring food to your apartment? What will she do if she sees me?"

172

"I'm going to tell her I have a cousin who's staying with me temporarily. You came in from the country to try to find work."

"I hope she believes you. If she doesn't, I hope she's on our side."

CHAPTER TWENTY-FIVE

The man behind the desk at the Registry Office was just as officious and record-conscious as a Nazi, but when Anton drew out his wallet and displayed two large bills, the process became easier. Finally, after much paperwork, the process was completed with the promise of bringing Alexandra in to sign the documents when she arrived for the wedding. Another trip to the wallet extracted a promise from the clerk that no notice of the wedding would appear in any paper.

Tereza's clothes were in bad shape. They'd been used garments, faded and worn, when Anna Havelkova had bought them at a thrift shop. Now they were in worse condition. The dress she'd worn to escape the palace had been ripped by the brick wall, and the hem was coming out. Since clothes were difficult to come by, he'd go to Teta Adelka. He thought she was the same size as Tereza, and she had closets full of clothes. In addition, he needed to find out whether Gustav was gone.

When he knocked on her door, she answered. "Zita's shopping for our supper. It's so good to see you." They went into the library.

"What's happened with Gustav?"

"He's gone."

"What happened? Someone came for him?"

She sat on the couch. He was sure she'd reveal as little as possible. "I don't know. When I got up yesterday morning, Zita told me he was gone. I didn't ask questions. Would you like some tea?"

"Yes, I'd like some. And I hope you won't be harboring any more fugitives."

"Of course not." She was smiling when she said it, and she left the room to make tea.

"Do you have a dress I can borrow, and some shoes?" he asked when she returned. "A friend's getting married, and the bride doesn't have a thing to wear. She's just your size." He couldn't tell anyone yet that he was getting married. How could he explain a wife who wasn't there, once she was extracted?

"I have lots of dresses, and I never go anywhere to wear them. Do you want a long dress?"

"No, it's a daytime wedding, a civil ceremony at this time. The church wedding will come later."

They went to her room and started through a closet. She reminisced over each dress, remembering the garden parties, dances, and operas she'd attended. Anton assured her she'd be doing those things again once the war was over.

"Here's a nice one for a simple civil ceremony," she said. It was olive green silk with a lace collar and cuffs. I think you should take a suit, too, in case the bride prefers it. A suit's always nice for that type wedding. I have a navy blue one here that would be perfect, and here's a lacy white blouse to go with it."

"Those two outfits will be fine. She'll have a choice. What about shoes?"

"This pair of black pumps would go with either outfit. But how do you know they'll fit?"

"I'm not sure, but I'll bring them back, anyway, whether they fit or not. She can try them. Do you have a suitcase I can carry these things in?"

She opened another closet. "Take your choice. I don't suppose I'll ever do any more traveling, so take one and keep it."

This would replace the one that was sitting uselessly in a locker at the train station, containing a Gestapo uniform without the jacket. "Thanks, Teta. You're most generous."

"So who's the friend that's getting married?"

"You wouldn't know him. He's a young attorney."

"What's his name? I might know him, or his family."

Damn, he should have been prepared for this. He said the first thing that popped into his head. "Neruda, Jan Neruda."

"Like the poet?"

"Yes."

" I wonder if he's related."

"He says he isn't. I'd better go. I promised to get these things to him."

"You can't stay and have a second cup of tea?"

"Well, maybe a bit more."

They sipped tea while he promised to take her to the opera and ballet once the madness ended. He kissed her cheek when he left and then walked back to Old Town and the same jewelry store where he once bought Eliska a diamond bracelet. Size five for the ring, she had said, and he found two simple gold bands that would be perfect for now.

#

He found the address on Skolska Street, went into a foyer, and climbed the stairs. His contact had specified the second floor, first door on he right, when he described the house. Anton went into the empty room and sat at a table that had several chairs surrounding it. He became concerned at two-fifteen, fearful that something had happened to his contact. This was the first time the man had failed to show up on time, and Anton was standing up to leave when he walked in.

"Sorry I'm late. An emergency developed that had to be taken care of."

"Anything to do with my aunt's boarder?"

"No, all went well there. This was something else."

The contact looked at the suitcase Anton had placed beside his chair. "Are you traveling?"

"No, just transferring some items from my aunt's house to my apartment."

"Others will be joining us. I've staggered the arrival times so it won't arouse suspicion in the neighborhood, so many people coming to the house at once."

Anton handed him the newspaper. I have a message that needs to be sent."

"About Tereza. I heard what happened."

"Yes."

The door opened shortly and the heavy-set man walked in, the man who had taught Anton about silent killing. After a twenty-minute interval, he was followed by Erik, and then Jakub. Another man arrived whom Anton didn't recognize, and finally, the man he knew as Alek Martinek.

"This is everyone," the contact said. "I'm sure most of you guessed this is about the Skoda Works. They're turning out more panzers now than ever before. Tomorrow night you'll blow up two railroad bridges on the Berounka. You'll be two teams of three. They have guards stationed at either end of the bridges. Two of you will take out the guards, and then the third will plant the explosives. We'll meet tomorrow just before dark." He looked at Anton. "You remember the house where you left Mr. Martinek?"

"Yes, I remember."

"You'll pick up Jakub and Erik on your way."

The heavy-set man shook his head. "There will be reprisals. None of us can forget Lidice."

"There may be reprisals, but this won't be viewed as seriously as the killing of the Reichsprotektor. And this is only the first of several planned events. How many of us can they kill?"

"Even one is too many."

"The destruction of the bridges will save lives. Not Czech lives, I'll admit, but it will help the Allies. Whatever we feel about it, we have our orders. And you'll be given final orders tomorrow evening when we meet again."

"If we're through, I'd like to leave first," Anton said. He walked out shortly after and returned to the apartment. Tereza was delighted with the clothes and wanted to try them on immediately. They decided on the suit, as the days were getting cooler now and she might need it for the warmth. The shoes were a little large, but they'd work with a little engineering. Anton kept the rings in his pocket. He'd save those for the ceremony.

He couldn't bear to destroy her excitement by telling her of his assignment. He would only hope he'd survive so their plans could be carried out.

CHAPTER TWENTY-SIX

The contact was the only person present in the living room of the farmhouse when Anton arrived with Jakub and Erik. The man handed him a book. "Have you heard of the poet Pablo Neruda?"

"No. Was he a relative of Jan?"

"No. He was from South America and had a Latin surname. I don't remember what it was, but he took the name Neruda because he admired Jan. He was a Communist, but I think you'll enjoy his poetry, nevertheless. You can keep the book—I bought it for you from a friend who needed money. Best to keep it hidden, though."

"Certainly, I'll keep it hidden. I keep all my books hidden, since it's difficult to know what's forbidden and what isn't. It was very kind of you to get it for me." He put the book in his knapsack, and they settled down to wait for the others. He had told Tereza that he had to be away for the night, and she hadn't asked questions; she simply had the look of concern on her face that he'd seen several times before.

Alek came from the back of he house and joined them, and the heavy-set man arrived shortly after with the tall stranger Anton had seen only at the house on Skolska Street.

"Anton, you and Erik will take Alek with you. He knows the way. You and Erik will take care of the guards, and Alek will set up the explosives. He needs to load some supplies into the trunk of your car. Bela will take the others in his car.

"We want the blasts to go off at the same time, at midnight. Let's synchronize our watches. It's now nine-seventeen."

Anton's watch showed nine-seventeen, and he wound it, just to be sure it would keep running. He couldn't help wishing Jakub were on his team rather than Erik. He realized this wish was selfish, but could he be blamed for wanting the best chance of surviving the night? On the other hand, he knew Erik's weaknesses and hoped he could anticipate problems.

They left in the Rosalie with Bela and the others following in a truck that Anton hadn't been able to identify in the dark. Alek directed him through the hills along country roads heading west just north of Pilsen. The headlights of the truck disappeared as they neared the Berounka.

"Turn in here," Alek said.

Anton drove into a lane that led to a house. There were no lights on.

"It's okay. We can leave the car here. It's about a mile to the bridge. We'll have to walk the rest of the way."

Alek took a large knapsack from the trunk and slung it on his back. They all carried boxes. Alek led them past the house and around a ridge through a heavily forested area. Once out of sight of the road, he took out a flashlight and showed the way.

After a while Anton could hear the river ahead. Alek turned off the flashlight. "No more noise," he said. "Anton, there's a path on the right that leads down to a footbridge across the river. You take that and come up behind the guard on the far side of the river. Erik will take care of the man on this side. Drag the bodies to the center of the bridge and come back here to wait."

Drag the bodies . . . Anton had been avoiding thinking about what he was about to do, but Alek's words brought him back to reality. He had killed the Gestapo officer in the Rosalie because he felt he had to do so in order to save their lives. Now he was going to sneak up behind an unsuspecting guard and plunge a knife between his ribs and deep into his chest. He reminded himself that the guard would kill him with no hesitation at all, given the chance. And slowing down the shipment of tanks from the Skoda Works undoubtedly would save lives somewhere.

He made his way down the riverbank, counting on the sound of the rushing water to cover any noises he made. He found the footbridge with the help of the halfmoon and walked across, holding the railing in case there were rotten boards underfoot. When he reached the other side, he started up the embankment, first through heavy weeds and then over the large gravel that formed the foundation for the railroad.

Above him, seated on a rail, he could see two figures. He swore under his breath. The smaller person, seated to the left of the guard, was a girl. Where in the devil had she come from? He could see the lights of a farmhouse about a mile downstream. She must have walked from there. She'd be screaming and would alert the other guard when he killed her companion. Then he heard a shot.

The guard and the girl stood up, looking toward the other end of the trestle. Anton knew he had to act and then try to figure out what had happened at the other end. He finished climbing the embankment with the knife in his hand. The guard was still staring at the other end, obviously trying to figure out what was happening, but the girl turned and looked at Anton. He curled his left arm around the guard, covering his mouth with his hand, and slid the knife through the thick fabric of the man's jacket and on into his chest. The guard sagged against him while making gasping noises in his throat. The girl screamed. Anton twisted the knife as he pulled it out.

"Go home. Get out of here," Anton whispered. He was suddenly angry with her for consorting with the enemy. "Don't ever do anything like this again, do you hear?" She nodded and stumbled down the track, sobbing, until she was out of sight in the darkness.

He didn't want to look at the guard, because he was probably very young if he was anything like the girl. He felt for a pulse; there was none. He couldn't see the other end of the trestle and decided it would be best to go back across the footbridge and up the other side.

When he climbed the embankment on the other side, he could see two figures lying on the ties between the rails. Both were silent, with no movement. He could see the knife in the guard's throat glinting in the moonlight. He reached for his arm and felt for a pulse, but there was none. He turned and knelt by Erik.

His chest was covered in coagulating blood. His hand reached toward Anton. Anton took him in his arms. "Hang on. We'll get you out of here and get help from Dr. Havelka."

"It's too late. Tell my parents . . ." He could say no more.

"I'll tell them you're a hero." Anton felt Erik go limp, and his breathing stopped. Anton sobbed and held Erik close. "I'll tell them you died a hero."

Tears were still running down Anton's cheeks as he retrieved Erik's knife and dragged the guards to the center of the trestle. He put Erik over his shoulder and made his way down the embankment and through the woods to the spot where they had parted with Alek, who wasn't there. Anton leaned Erik's body against a tree and sat down beside him. Alek would be setting up the explosives. Anton looked at his watch and saw that it was twenty minutes till midnight.

It was two minutes after when he heard the explosion. He couldn't help wondering if it was worth it, losing Erik and with reprisals sure to follow.

#

He left Erik's body in the trunk and walked to the door of his parents' house. When he took Alek to the farmhouse where he lived, the lady of the house had insisted they clean the blood from Erik's body and dress him in clean clothes. She insisted Anton do the same, and she kept the bloody garments to use in some future venture, he guessed. His legs felt like lead as he approached the house.

Erik's father answered Anton's knock. "I regret to tell you that Erik was killed last night. If it's any consolation, your son died a hero."

The man was looking at Anton with a mixture of hatred and fear on his face. "Where is his body?"

"In the trunk of the car. I'll bring him in for you."

"I'll carry him to the house. Get out, and don't ever come back here."

As he drove toward Prague, Anton could think of nothing but the consolation he'd find in Tereza's arms.

#

The message said, "Meet contact Ceske Budejovice lobby Grand Hotel Zvon. Seven pm Saturday. Contact phrase are you enjoying the hotel." They had five days. Tereza was reading over his shoulder. Also in the book were all the documents she'd need for traveling to Ceske Budejovice.

Anton laid the papers aside. "Let's get married tomorrow morning. I think we should take the train to Ceske Budejovice immediately after. We can go directly to the station from City Hall. We'll stay at the Grand Hotel Zvon and have a short honeymoon before you have to go."

She looked as if she might cry at his talk of going, and she didn't say anything for a moment. Then she smiled. "I'd love that. An actual honeymoon."

They packed that evening, using the small suitcase Teta Adelka had given him and Tereza's knapsack. She'd need to take that with her on the plane. When they woke up the next morning, they dressed quickly and went to City Hall. The man who had issued their license came in with another employee from his office to witness the wedding. Anton stood at Tereza's side and tried to forget the war, the resistance, the turmoil of his life. She was all that mattered at the moment, and he would make the most of it. They hurried to the train station when the ceremony was over and made it just in time for the train to Ceske Budejovice.

Gestapo officers checked their documents and found them satisfactory. "It's lucky that Prague is full of pretty blondes," he whispered when they were alone in their compartment. "You're the prettiest one of all, of course."

She snuggled against him. "I'm determined to make the most of our time together. I'm determined not to cry."

#

They sat in the lobby of the Grand Hotel Zvon and watched the fountain splashing in the square. At seven o'clock a woman approached and sat down beside Tereza. "Are you enjoying the hotel?"

"It's lovely," Tereza said.

He hadn't expected a woman, who now looked at him and said, "You'll have to tell her goodbye now. She has to leave with me."

"I'm going with her as far as I can. I assume she's flying out?"

The woman was reluctant to give him the information, but finally said, "Yes, she'll be flying."

"I'm going with her to the field. I want to see her get on that plane."

"My orders are to take her, and that you'll be staying here."

Other people had caused enough complications for him in this business, and now it was his turn to cause some. "She's not going unless I go with her. Then you will bring me back here, and I'll leave from here tomorrow morning to go back to Prague." Of course he didn't mean that. She had to get out, regardless. It was a bluff.

"Okay, then you're going."

Tereza patted his hand. Now she was near tears. She was wearing the wedding suit.

"I have some warmer clothes in the truck that you're to change into when we get to the field. Do you have everything you want to take with you in the knapsack?

"It's all in here. We're ready to go."

They walked to the rear of the hotel, where the woman had parked an ancient and dusty Praga AN. They climbed aboard the truck, and the woman drove a few miles to a landing field that had been cleared in the middle of the woods. It reminded Anton of the one where she had landed, except this one didn't have a tree in the middle. It was dark by the time they arrived, and four torches burned on each side of the field. Tereza had changed into long underwear under boy's jeans, and she was wearing a sweater with a parka over it.

They kissed, and their driver turned away to give them a private moment. They heard the Lysander a few minutes before it arrived. It landed with only feet to spare. The three of them would have cheered, but they were cautious about making noise. The pilot managed to turn it, and they all walked to the end of the runway. Anton and Tereza kissed again. "I'll try to send you food," she said. "I'll be back so fast when the war ends . . ."

"I'll be waiting for you. Be safe. Don't worry about food; just take care of yourself."

"You too. I love you." She climbed into the plane and the canopy closed over her.

CHAPTER TWENTY-SEVEN

General Bill Donovan was even more imposing in person that he was in the photos she'd seen of him. He looked through a folder, which she assumed was hers, and then looked up at her. "We appreciate the work you did for us in Prague. It's a shame it had to end so soon, but you did what you had to do. The keys you took when you left are proving to be most useful." He leaned back in his chair and smiled at her across the desk. "I hear you're married now."

She was surprised that he already knew this. "Yes, sir."

"For the time being we're going to keep you here at headquarters, in the Research and Analysis Division. Your language skills make you a valuable asset for us, both in the field and in the office. There's a young woman who's living in a two-bedroom apartment on Dupont Circle, where you stayed before, and we've arranged for you to share with her for the time being. It's within walking distance."

Alexandra—she was back to thinking of herself as Alexandra—left OSS headquarters with all the necessary security documents she'd need for reporting to work the next morning. She walked to the address Gen. Donovan had given her and was pleased with the neat appearance of the row house. She was directed to the second floor by a lady who was sweeping the hallway of the first. She knocked on the door of apartment number three on the right side of the hallway and got no answer. Her roommate wasn't home. She let herself into the apartment with the key the general had given her.

The apartment was neat but sparsely furnished. The first bedroom she looked into had an ornate silver mirror, comb and brush set and a blue bottle of Evening in Paris cologne on the dresser. She closed the door and checked the other room, which had an empty dresser, a bed, and a night stand. She unpacked her few belongings and put them in the dresser drawers. She'd need to shop this afternoon for a couple of outfits that would do until her mother mailed some clothes.

A window across from the foot of her bed looked out onto the circle, and she drew back the lace curtain. If only Anton were here with her at this window, looking out onto the beautiful circle and sharing the apartment with her, life would be perfect. Everything she heard or saw reminded her of him; it was useless to try to shake the longing that nagged at her constantly. It would be with her till she returned to Prague.

CHAPTER TWENTY-EIGHT

Three weeks had passed since Tereza's departure, and Anton was missing her more than ever. He was resigned to staying busy, if not with underground affairs, then at the office. Even though his law practice had dwindled since he joined the underground and began neglecting his career, he had enough work to keep his mind occupied, at least during the daytime. It was the evenings that took him to near despair, wondering how long the war would last, wondering whether either of them would survive it.

He tried to dwell on the positive news he'd had in the last three weeks. Both railroad bridges had been blown up, bridges on the route that carried tanks from the Skoda Munitions Works to the German front. He had gone to the Kolkovna the day after and found Jakub back at work. All three members of his team had survived.

He heard even better news when his contact called him for a meeting at the Café Slavia. The man was reading a paper, and he put it down when Anton approached. Was it word that Tereza had arrived safely in Washington? He had refused to let himself consider any other possibility since he had been summoned to the meeting the day before.

The contact motioned for the waiter. "Please refill my coffee, and bring some for Mr. Janak."

Anton sat down. "Any word about Tereza?"

"You'll be happy to hear that she's in Washington, in an apartment, and she's going to be working at headquarters for the time being."

Anton put his hands over his face, and tears seeped out from under his eyelids. He brushed them away. "Thank God." He barely had control of his voice.

The waiter was approaching. "I have nothing else for you at the moment," the contact said, "so let's relax and enjoy our coffee."

They had discussed the poetry of Pablo Neruda, which Anton had read since the contact gave him the book. Anton had wondered from the beginning whether his contact was a Communist, and he became surer of it all the time. The fight against the Nazis had made strange bedfellows, but this was something to be sorted out when the war was over.

#

He had walked by Tereza's apartment twice since she had been gone. They had discussed the loss of her bicycle and lace tablecloth. Now Anton decided he'd try to retrieve the items. The rental had been made in the name of his law firm, and Tereza had given the address of another older apartment building when she went to work at the palace, so there was no reason to think the Nazis would know about the place—unless someone had followed her home, that is. Anton had terminated the rental agreement on the phone; now he decided he should try to remove her things from the apartment before the month was over.

He walked by the place on Saturday morning and went on to a café around the corner from her building. After a roll and tea, he came back and went down the stairs. He let himself in and saw she had made her bed neatly before going to work that day. She had washed a few dishes, and they were propped on a dish towel beside the sink. He put them in the cabinet and then folded the towel and put it in a drawer. He'd leave the sheets—they must have come with the apartment.

He found the linen tablecloth she longed for in the top drawer of her dresser. He put it in the bottom of his knapsack and piled the clothes from the drawers in on top. He'd keep the tablecloth at his apartment and take the clothes to Dr. Havelka's and leave them with Anna. Maybe she'd find another use for them in the future. The books he'd brought so that Tereza could practice reading Czech went into the bag also.

Tereza had been keeping a diary, but it wasn't in the dresser. Did she have it with her on the day she had to escape from the palace? He hadn't thought to mention it. Maybe it was in Washington with her. He looked in all the cabinets and then went to the bathroom. The diary was there at the back of a drawer, behind a washcloth and towel. He slipped it into the knapsack. They'd read it together after the war.

He was overcome by nostalgia as he left, looking back at the table where they'd sipped tea and shared the Nazi's pastries and at the bed where they'd made love.

#

Getting the bicycle would be trickier, but he wanted to surprise her with it when she returned to Prague. It had been almost a month—maybe it would be gone, but he was determined to try. He had seen where she parked it on the morning he went to the palace to give testimony about the death of Frederich Hesse. She left it chained in a small stand of trees beside the road. Winter was coming on, and it would be best to get the bicycle before the leaves fell from the trees and left him more open to exposure.

He decided he should go after the bicycle during the day with an air of insouciance. Mrs. Svobodova's husband had left a box of tools in the garage when he deserted her, and Anton found a bolt cutter and put it into his knapsack. He walked into the trees as he went up the hill toward the palace, and on into the area where Tereza parked the bicycle. It was still there, leaning against a young beech tree. He walked to it, took out the bolt cutter, and cut the chain. He put both the cutter and chain in his knapsack and noticed that the front tire was flat. He'd have to push the bike all the way to his apartment.

Someone was coming down the road—he could see movement through the trees. He moved farther into the grove. He could see now that it was a woman, and she entered the trees and headed for the bicycle. She stood there looking at it for a moment, and then looked around. "Hello! Is someone there?" She said the words softly.

He came from behind a large tree and headed toward her.

"I'm Olga," she said. "I'm a friend of the bicycle owner."

Anton nodded. "So am I."

"I noticed the chain was cut, so I thought I might find someone here, someone who could tell me if she's okay."

Olga must be the contact inside the palace. "She's okay. She went home for a while. She'll be back when conditions improve. I'll keep her bicycle for her till then."

Olga's lower lip trembled, and a tear rolled down her cheek. "Thank you." She turned and went back to the road, and he could see her walking on down the hill.

He'd wait a while till she was gone before he started down. He had to leave before the other workers were through, however, since one of them might know it was Tereza's bicycle, perhaps someone who was a collaborator. He gave Olga ten minutes to reach the bottom of the hill, and then made his way through the trees till he had to move to the road.

The Charles Bridge was crowded, but no one paid any attention to a man with a knapsack who was pushing a bicycle. He passed a group of Gestapo on their way to a café for an afternoon break, and they looked at him as if he were another poor Czech forced to push his lame bicycle.

When he reached his garage, he had to back the Rosalie out in order to take the bicycle in. He rummaged through the toolbox and found a hammer and some nails, and he pounded two into the studs at the end of the garage. The bicycle would hang there till Tereza returned. It would be best to fix the tire just before she came back to Prague. Maybe, if the war was over, he could get a new tire.

What next? Something, anything, to keep busy. He had the tools; he had nails. He would fix the stairs to his apartment, make them more stable. He was no carpenter, but could it be that difficult? And after that, Teta Adelka needed to have some boards replaced in her porch floor, if he could get the lumber. Maybe Mrs. Svobodova had something that needed to be repaired at the shop. He would learn to work with his hands by doing it.

Tereza would be proud that he had devoted himself to constructive endeavors while waiting out the war for her return. She wouldn't want him to give in to despair, and the thought of her return would keep him from it. What was it Pablo Neruda had said? Something like, "You can cut all the flowers, but you can't keep spring from coming."

BIOGRAPHY

Helen Haught Fanick's short stories have appeared in *Women's Household, Midnight Zoo, Vermont Ink*, and in various anthologies and online publications. Her articles and photos have been published in *Texas Observer, Stepping Stones*, and other periodicals. Her poem, *Leaf Fall*, was published in *Nature's Gifts*, an anthology to benefit The Nature Conservancy. She has won several local and state awards, and two national awards in the Writer's Digest Competition.

Helen's novel, Moon Signs, was a quarter-finalist in the 2011 Amazon Breakthrough Novel Awards. The second novel in the Moon Mystery Series, Moonlight Mayhem, and a collection of three short stories, Bad Moon Rising, were published in January 2012. All three publications are available through Amazon. Saving Susie, a suspense novel, reached the second level of the 2012 Amazon Breakthrough Novel Awards and was published in March 2012, and City Life, another suspense novel, was published July 2012.

Helen is a graduate of The University of Texas at San Antonio with a degree in English and lives in San Antonio with her husband.

Made in the USA
Lexington, KY
16 February 2019